PRAISE FOR
SCRITCH SCRATCH

"*Scritch Scratch* brims with eerie thrills and nail-biting chills that are sure to keep readers turning pages. Don't dare read this at night!"

—Kate Hannigan, author of
the League of Secret Heroes series

"Delightfully chilling and rooted in history, this haunting thrill ride will keep you hooked."

—Jess Keating, author of *Nikki Tesla
and the Ferret-Proof Death Ray*

"A spooky mystery with a sweet heart. Readers will be gripped by Currie's storytelling, and encouraged and excited to look into the history of their own cities and towns."

—Jarrett Lerner, author of the EngiNerds series

SCRITCH SCRATCH

SCRITCH
SCRATCH

LINDSAY CURRIE

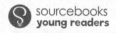

Published by Sourcebooks Young Readers, an imprint of Sourcebooks Kids
P.O. Box 4410, Naperville, Illinois 60567-4410
(630) 961-3900
sourcebookskids.com

Library of Congress Cataloging-in-Publication Data

Names: Currie, Lindsay, author.
Title: Scritch scratch / Lindsay Currie.
Description: Naperville, IL : Sourcebooks Young Readers, [2020] | Audience:
   Ages 10-14. | Audience: Grades 7-9. | Summary: Haunted after helping her
   father on his ghost-themed Chicago bus tour, twelve-year-old Claire must
   discover what the spectral boy from the bus wants before it is too late.
Identifiers: LCCN 2020005286 | (hardcover)
Subjects: CYAC: Ghosts--Fiction | Family life--Illinois--Chicago--Fiction.
   | Friendship--Fiction. | Eastland (Ship)--Fiction. |
   Shipwrecks--Fiction. | Chicago (Ill.)--Fiction. | Mystery and detective
   stories.
Classification: LCC PZ7.C9354 Scr 2020 | DDC [Fic]--dc23
LC record available at https://lccn.loc.gov/2020005286

This product conforms to all applicable CPSC and CPSIA standards.

Source of Production: LSC Communications, Harrisonburg, Virginia, United States
Date of Production: July 2020
Run Number: 5018857

Printed and bound in the United States of America.
LSC 10 9 8 7 6 5 4 3 2 1

To my son, Rob.

May the next year be an adventure

as wonderful and brilliant as you are.

Go Blue!

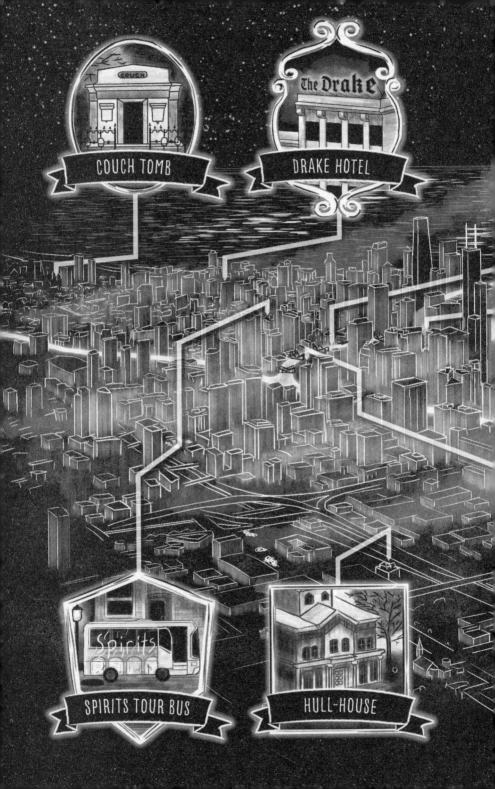

SS EASTLAND

ALLEY OF DEATH

RESURRECTION MARY

CONGRESS HOTEL

CONGRESS HOTEL

ONE

If someone had told me yesterday that I'd be spending my Saturday morning in the aisle of a stuffy bookstore searching for ghost stories, I would've told them they were nuts. But here I am, staring down an entire row of books with titles like *Windy City Mysteries, Chi-Town Haunts,* and *Second City Ghosts.*

I guess I should've expected this. Having a dad who is interested in creepy Chicago history is one thing, but having a dad who is *obsessed* with it is another thing altogether. Two years ago, he wrote a mystery novel called *Spirits of Chicago.* He went on a book tour and even did an interview on the local news station. I was cool with it at first, but when he announced to the family that he was quitting his job teaching history to start a tour bus company, things went sideways. See, it wasn't just any tour bus company. It was a *ghost* tour bus company.

Seriously.

Ghost tours.

So it's no big shocker that we're standing in this bookstore instead of going home. Dad is drawn to this kind of stuff. The dark. The sinister. The *ghostly*.

I prefer beakers and test tubes to gravestones and mausoleums. Science is predictable. Comforting. It's something you can see, hear, touch, and smell—unlike Dad's "ghosts."

"The boulder isn't even placed over Kennison's actual burial site," Dad mutters to no one in particular. This is how he gets when he's researching. It's more like a trance than anything, so usually I just leave him alone. Only today it's hard. This place could put a Mountain Dew addict to sleep.

A giggle breaks the silence. I swivel my head, looking for my best friend, Casley. That was her giggle; I'm sure of it. I start to walk in the direction I *think* the laughter came from, but I stop in my tracks when I realize she isn't alone. Staying behind a bookshelf, I watch Cas flip through the pages of a graphic novel while Emily Craig reads over her shoulder. They burst into laughter more than once, the sound of their happiness needling me. I ease farther behind the bookshelf and force myself to breathe through the ache in my stomach. Cas didn't invite me to hang out with them; she didn't even mention it.

Emily just moved here a couple of months ago, but Casley has been hanging out with her more and more lately. Inviting her to sit at our lunch table, begging her to join the science club, including her on group texts. There's nothing wrong with Emily; I mean, she seems nice enough. But she's quiet when I'm around. Casley swears it's nothing. I'm not so sure. I guess I get it; Emily and I don't have anything in common. She's into stuff Cas and I have never been into before. Makeup. Hair products. Clothes. Now that Casley seems to be into these things, too, I feel like I don't belong whenever the three of us are together.

"Dad," I whisper, rounding the corner where my father is still standing, nose in a book. "Can we go now?"

He slowly flips a page, then immediately turns it back as if he might have missed something. I drop my face into my hands and groan. The longer we stay here, the more likely it is that Cas will see me. Even worse, she might think I'm spying on her.

"Dad!" I hiss louder, ignoring the pointed stare of a man shuffling past. "I have to work on my science fair project. Can you just buy the book so we can go home?"

Dad looks up, blinking at me as if he has just remembered I'm here. He probably has.

"Oh. Sure thing, Claire. Let me check out really quick, and I'll get you home."

I scan the aisles nervously, suddenly aware that Casley's laughter has quieted down. Maybe they left. Peeking around the bookshelf at the register, I groan at my bad luck. Not only is Casley still here, she's buying something.

Dad heaves his enormous messenger bag off the floor and taps on the cover of the book he's holding. The picture on the front is of several men in suits smoking cigars and leaning against a brick wall. The word *massacre* is printed across the lower half of the photo in a shocking red that looks like it's dripping down the page.

I wince. "Is that supposed to be blood?"

"It's about a Mob hit in the 1920s where seven men died, so I would assume so," Dad says with a dry chuckle. "I've never considered making the site of the Saint Valentine's Day Massacre part of the tour, but this book might have changed my mind. There's been quite a lot of paranormal activity documented there. Plus, the site is so close. Practically right next to your school!"

Next to my school? My skin bristles uncomfortably. I've learned a lot over the last two years about our neighborhood, Lincoln Park, and unfortunately, it's all bad. Unlike most parents, Dad doesn't focus on *normal* Chicago history when he tells stories. Forget protests and pioneers and famous residents. Instead, it's always some nightmarish tragedy that left behind an angry, restless spirit (or several). Whatever. Dad's stories used to scare me, but that was back before I was into science and knew how fake all this stuff is.

"Ready to hit the road?" He nudges me toward the cashier with a conspiratorial grin, as if I'm just as excited about his new book as he is. Little does he know that I'd rather eat the book than read it.

"Mm-hmm," I mumble, slowly picking my bag up off the floor to waste time. If Dad rushes for the checkout line right now, he'll run straight into Cas. He'll show her the book. He might even start talking about his ghost tours, and even though Casley is used to it, Emily isn't. No matter how nice Casley thinks she is, she'll start rumors. New people always do.

Slinging my bag over my shoulder, I snatch the book from Dad's hands. "You can get this cheaper online."

Dad looks like he's been slapped. "You know I don't like shopping online, Claire! That is driving bookstores like this out of business!"

Darn. If this store goes out of business, it will be one less place for Dad to embarrass us. "I'm just saying that if you want the book, you could get it tomorrow for way less by doing that."

Please listen. Please try to hear what I'm actually saying. Please, please, please.

Dad shoves his glasses up his nose and gives me a stern

look. Reaching over, he pries my fingers off the book one at a time. "The price is fine, Little Miss Cheapskate. Let's go."

Just when I think I have no choice but to trip him or fake an injury of my own to slow him down, I hear the jingle of the small bell above the door. Someone left! Trotting to the window, I exhale in relief. It was Casley. She skips away from the store, one willowy arm linked through Emily's like a fence—a fence meant to keep me out.

TWO

It's eleven fifteen when Dad and I get back home. He drops me off on the sidewalk out front, then drives away to find a decent parking spot—something that's harder than bathing a cat. I love Chicago, but our neighborhood is crowded, especially on the weekends. We don't own a garage, so my parents spend a lot of time swearing while trying to cram our ancient minivan into parking spots meant for way smaller cars.

I spent the entire drive home trying to recover from seeing Casley at the bookstore, but I don't feel better. My heart is still racing, and I'm still mad. Not just at Casley, but at Dad, too. Doesn't he understand that his stupid ghost tour bus is terrible for me? Middle school is all about blending in, but he's doing his best to make me stick out.

Pinching the bridge of my nose, I try to focus on the good

stuff. I have the perfect evening planned, an evening that will make all my worries go away. For now, at least. As soon as Dad leaves for his tour and Mom takes Sam to hockey, I'm going to put on my fuzzy slippers, make a mug of hot chocolate, and brainstorm my science fair project.

Unless Casley calls me and invites me over. As much as I love the science fair, that would be better for sure. Most Saturday nights, we curl up with a bowl of candy and watch movies or come up with new ways to earn money for our microscope fund. We've mowed lawns, shoveled snow, and even walked dogs, and after almost a year, we're only one hundred dollars short. Unfortunately, something tells me we won't be doing that tonight. I check my phone for the zillionth time. No missed calls, no texts. Nothing.

Maybe Cas decided to have a sleepover with Emily instead. My heart aches at the thought.

I trudge toward the gate that secures the narrow alley between my building and the neighboring one, then pause. I hate the alley, especially when it's empty. Metal dumpsters, rats scurrying in the shadows, and the constant smell of something rotting. But since I misplaced my key to the front door a long time ago, I'm stuck using the back entrance. That means this stinky alley and I need to get along somehow.

There are exactly fifty-four steps from the gate to the

back door. Dragging my keys from around my neck, I unlock the gate. A dank, musty smell fills my nose.

"Thirteen...fourteen...fifteen..." I focus on counting as I make my way past the first set of dumpsters. A faint scurrying behind one of them makes my hands go clammy. *It's just an alley, Claire. If you can memorize the entire periodic table, you can handle this*, I remind myself. But it doesn't help much, because the periodic table is nothing like this. It may be challenging to remember, but it isn't dirty or scary or smelly. It's fascinating. A squeaking sound echoes off the brick walls around me.

"Sixteen...seventeen...eighteen..." My voice is shaking now. What was that sound?

"Nineteen...twenty..." Someone whispers from the shadows at the far end of the alley. It's a raspy sound—a terrifying one. Screaming, I spin back toward the gate.

"Jeez, Claire, stop! It's just me! What the heck?"

I freeze. My legs still want to run, but my brain stops them. The voice is familiar. I turn around slowly. Sam walks out from behind the dumpster closest to the back door. He's clutching his stomach and laughing.

"Sam?" I sputter. He must have come out of the basement when I wasn't looking. "You scared me!"

My jerk of a brother comes closer. His messy brown hair is jammed up beneath a Cubs hat, and his mouth is curled into a smirk. Not just a smirk—*the* smirk. The one that makes me want to kick him where it counts. Someone at school once said younger brothers are the worst, but I disagree. Older brothers win, hands down.

Balling up a piece of paper, Sam shoves it into his pocket. "That scream was brutal. Jumpy much?"

I gesture to the dumpsters. "Can you blame me? This place is freaky."

"So, let me get this straight. You're voluntarily part of a club at school where someone caught their hair on fire last year, but you're scared of the alley?" He scoffs.

"It was only her bangs, and she barely singed them!" I cross my arms over my chest and scowl at him. "What were you doing hiding back there, anyway? Were you just waiting to scare me?"

"Yeah, I spend all my Saturdays hunched behind a smelly dumpster."

I make a face at him. His sarcasm is endless. And irritating.

He rolls his eyes. "No, brainiac. I was not waiting for you. I was just leaving and saw you down here. Why were you counting, anyway?"

Ugh. Sam is the last person I want to know that I need to count out loud to get through this alley. He'll never let me forget it. "None of your business."

"Whatever you say. I'm leaving. Need me to walk you to the back door, or you gonna be okay, widdle girl?"

"Shut up," I snap. As much as I'd like company, I'd rather let a Yeti walk me than my annoying brother. "I'm fine."

"Suit yourself," Sam says, and the gate slams shut behind him, leaving me alone in the alley again. I hesitate for a moment and then race the remaining thirty-six steps to the back door.

THREE

The house is quiet when I walk in. Even the oven looks empty, and with Mom's online bakery business—JuliCakes—just starting to take off, it's pretty much never empty.

I've just wandered into the living room when I hear Mom's voice. It rises and falls, the timbre becoming more strained with every second that passes. Curious, I creep over to Dad's office door and press an ear against it. Muffled *mm-hmm*s filter through the thick wood, followed by a clear sigh. The door suddenly opens, and I lose my balance. You'd think I would be less clumsy after the three years of dance Mom insisted I take when I was younger, but no. I hit the hard wooden floor with all the grace of a three-legged donkey.

"Claire? What in the world?" Mom holds out a hand to

help me up. She's wearing a light blue apron with hearts on it today.

I must look just as shocked as she does, because her eyes soften. "Honey, are you okay?"

"Yeah. For sure." If Mom suspects that I was listening in on her conversation, she doesn't show it. "Sorry about that."

Mom smiles and pulls me into a hug. It makes me warm on the inside. Some moms wear perfume and fancy lotions to make them smell good, but not mine. Julia Koster always smells like a little slice of heaven because of her baking. I'd take the smell of a freshly baked chocolate chip cookie over a fancy lotion any day.

I look around the room. It's empty. It's also as messy as always. Stacks of manuscripts lining the desk. Pens and pencils scattered everywhere. An explosion of Post-it Notes on the floor. My father has got to be the most disorganized writer in the world.

"So, um, everything okay?" I ask.

Mom's lips turn downward, and I notice the dusting of white powder in her hair. Probably flour. Mom may smell good, but sometimes she looks like the kitchen attacked her.

"Dad just called. Minor setback."

"What's wrong? No parking?"

"Ugh, I wish it were just parking. Joshua is very sick and

had to cancel for tonight," Mom says, lifting a hand to rub her temple. I didn't notice before, but she looks exhausted. Her blond hair is falling out of its bun in messy chunks, and she's got her glasses on instead of contacts. "Without him, I don't know what your father is going to do."

Joshua. It takes a minute for the name to sink in, but once it does, I get why Mom is frowning. Joshua is the tour driver. He navigates the bus to all the "haunted" spots while Dad recites facts about them.

"Oh. So Dad will have to drive?" I ask. "No biggie. He knows the route, right?"

Mom nods, and the worried lines deepen around her eyes. "Yes, but Joshua does more than drive, kiddo. He collects receipts, keeps the tour moving on schedule, hands out brochures... It's quite a serious problem that he can't work tonight."

"Dad could do that stuff," I offer. Maybe it would make the night more hectic, but I still don't get why this is that big of a deal.

"He could, but there's nowhere to park at some of the stops."

I lift a questioning eyebrow at her.

"Nowhere *legal*," Mom corrects. "That means someone has to keep an eye on the bus while your Dad takes the passengers out to look around." She laughs ruefully. "You know how fast cars get parking tickets around here. A bus that size would get fined in a heartbeat!"

"Can't he just cancel tonight's tour?"

"No. It's unprofessional to cancel on customers this late. They'd definitely be upset." Mom looks thoughtful. "Plus, he would have to refund everyone."

Oh. This is about money. Considering how much time my parents spend worrying about how they'll get all the bills paid around here, I shouldn't be surprised. They might not think I hear them talking about it, but the walls are thin in this place. Most nights, I could repeat their conversations word for word. Dad worrying about making enough money with the tour bus and his writing. Mom worrying that her online bakery is costing more than it earns. It makes me sad to think that doing the things they love is so hard. It also makes me dread adulthood.

I perk up as an idea comes to me. "Hey, Sam is always begging Dad to let him ride along. Can't he skip the game and do Joshua's other jobs? Just for one night?"

Deep down, I know this is the *worst* possible option. Sam isn't like me; he isn't responsible. But I don't like the other direction this is going.

"Sam has back-to-back hockey games," Mom answers.

"Even if he wasn't their only goalie, it wouldn't be right to leave the team a player short for two games."

So, Sam can't do it, and neither can Mom. That just leaves...

Her concerned eyes glide to me and pause. "You know we wouldn't ask you if there were any other choice, right?"

My jaw drops.

"Just hear me out," Mom starts, holding her palms up, her fingers spread wide like I'm a wild animal about to attack. "It's only one night. Two and a half hours. Plus, Dad says he'll pay you fifty dollars. It would be a nice addition to your microscope fund!"

I hold a hand up to stop her from saying anything else. No. The answer is no. I'd love to add money to the microscope fund, but I *hate* the tour bus.

"I can't." I say it as firmly as I can without getting in trouble. Mom is pretty chill, but she has her limits. "I have to work on my science fair project."

She crosses her arms over her chest and gives me an *I'm not buying it* look. "The fair isn't for more than a month, Claire. Besides, aren't you pairing up with Casley this year? That should mean you have less to do on your own, right?"

Wrong. Casley and I were going to team up for the science fair this year, but she doesn't seem all that interested these days. In fact, I'm beginning to think she forgot about it entirely. I don't want to admit this to Mom—to *anyone*—just yet, so I simply shake my head.

"I know it seems like there's a lot of time, but I want to win again. I can't do that if I don't have time to work on it."

Small pricks of sweat break out on my forehead despite the chill in the air. I'm losing this argument, I can feel it. All I want is to be normal, to be able to talk about my family at school without kids hiding laughter behind their hands or whispering about us when they think I'm not listening. This— spending my night on Dad's tour bus—is going to make that even harder. *Especially* if someone sees me. Someone like Warner Jameson. He's got brown hair that always looks a little ruffled and grayish eyes that remind me of Lake Michigan on a stormy day. Not only is he cute, he's nice. When everyone else was gossiping about me last year, telling stories about my dad believing in ghosts and holding séances, he didn't. He didn't even laugh.

I've liked him ever since.

Mom shifts the stuff on Dad's desk around until she uncovers a worn notebook. She hands it to me, her expression serious. "This is the information you'll need to know for tonight. Look over it, please, because your father will need you ready to leave here by five."

I open my mouth to respond, but she presses the notebook into my hands. It feels heavy and terrible. Like a warning. "I'm sorry, sweetie. We know this isn't ideal, but your father and I are out of options."

Right. Out of options. My stomach coils into a knot. This tour is going to be the worst two and a half hours of my life.

FOUR

Dad's tour bus picks up its passengers downtown on Clark Street. The street is loud and busy, all bright lights and honking car horns. Good thing the tour is scheduled to leave soon, because this part of the city could give a girl a headache quick.

I scan the area, noticing that a massive travel bus is parked along the side of the street. Its windows are darkly tinted, but there's no sign of my father's ridiculous logo on it. "Is that it?"

Dad nods. "It is indeed. Joshua usually picks it up and drives it here, but fortunately I have a good relationship with the rental company, so they were kind enough to bring it down here for me today. I'll just go sign their paperwork and grab the keys."

Dad trots off, and I let out the breath I've been holding, relieved. It would be almost impossible for any of my class-mates to see me through those tinted windows. Plus, without any words or logos, it looks like it could be any kind of bus. There's no way to tell it apart from the ones that do those celebrity homes tours, or even those boring architecture tours. Maybe I'm not doomed tonight after all!

I do a little fist pump. For once, something is going right. I'll still be miserable tonight, but at least I can be miserable without anyone knowing. What's the word for that? Incognito?

Dad returns, keys in hand. The smile on his face is a mile wide. "All set!"

"Okay." I open the bag he saddled me with as we got into the car and paw through the brochures. "So, I'm supposed to give one to everyone, right?"

"Yup. You'll take their receipt, hand them a brochure that will detail all our stops tonight, then instruct them to take any seat they'd like. Meanwhile, I'll be just inside the bus, familiar-izing myself with all the passengers as they come on. I like to get to know them a little over the course of the evening, make them feel at home."

Huh. Ghost-chasing misfits are the last people I would want to "get to know," but then again, this *is* my dad we're talking about.

"Oh, and be pleasant, Claire," he adds sternly. "I know you wanted to hang out with your friends tonight instead of this, but I don't want my passengers to know that."

I grumble a quiet *okay*, irritated by his cluelessness. I wasn't planning to hang out with my friends tonight. Thanks to Emily, it wasn't even an option!

"I also need you to motion to me at every stop when we are exactly five minutes away from our departure time. Five minutes—no more, no less. That's my cue to wrap up any final thoughts and take questions."

"Five minutes. Got it," I repeat, doing my best to sound professional. I don't know why I want to impress Dad tonight, or ever, but I do. I guess I don't like to disappoint people, even if they disappoint me.

"Lastly, but perhaps most importantly, don't forget this rule: No tour guest is allowed on the bus alone. It's a liability."

I've heard the word *liability* before, and I think it has something to do with lawsuits, so I nod my head gravely.

"All right, enough of the ground rules. This is the first time you've seen the bus, right?" Dad asks, his eyes brightening.

My gaze wanders back to the bus. "Yeah."

He rubs his hands together, either from cold or excitement. "It's great, huh? Wish I could say I own it. Don't worry, though. We can still personalize it a little bit."

Uh-oh. Personalize? My stomach plummets.

Reaching into his messenger bag, Dad pulls out what looks like an enormous roll of plastic. He slowly unfurls it against the side of the bus until it lies flat.

"Ta-da!" he shouts, a wild, toothy grin stretched across his face. "Isn't this amazing?"

My eyes settle on the word SPIRITS, the eerie letters perched on top of a squat row of gravestones. The letters are distorted and grow slightly fainter at the tops, almost as if they are rising up from the graves themselves. Like spirits.

Gah. I've seen Dad's logo on the computer and on letterhead dozens of times, but this is the biggest, ugliest version I've ever seen. I squint at it, half-tempted to cover my eyes. "It's so... ahh...bright."

Dad nods excitedly. "Yes! That's because it isn't just any logo. It's a glow-in-the-dark logo!"

"Glow-in-the-dark?" I whimper. "Really?"

"Yup! All my tours are after dark, and a regular old logo wouldn't be visible enough. And even better...I have two! One for each side!"

It's official. I'm going to die of embarrassment tonight.

"Let's get this other one stuck to the side of the bus before the passengers arrive, shall we?" Dad holds one out for me to take.

Eyeing it, I hesitate. "Couldn't that mess up the bus? Like, leave marks on the sides or something?"

Dad laughs and waves me off. "Don't worry about that— it's static cling! Peels right off at the end of the night."

Great. We might as well tattoo the logo on our foreheads, too.

The wind whips around the corners of the buildings, making me shiver. I begin smoothing my logo out on the side, my mood sinking like a deflated balloon. So much for being incognito. These logos are going to let all of Chicago know *exactly* what kind of bus this is.

Pulling my baseball cap out of my bag, I tug it down low over my face. A few tendrils of my light brown hair have pulled loose from my scrunchie, but I don't care. As long as no one recognizes me, I'm good.

FIVE

The first passengers arrive about ten minutes later. As expected, they are a *bizarre* bunch. One woman is wearing something that looks suspiciously like a toga. Another lady is wearing sunglasses. At night. The man standing just to the right of me is snapping picture after picture of the tour bus with the lens cap still on his camera.

Careful to keep my cap low, I dutifully collect receipts and hand out brochures. Once I've checked off the last name from the list Dad gave me, I nod to him through the window, then begin stuffing the receipts into a large, orange envelope. My eyes land on the dollar amount at the bottom of one. Sixty-eight dollars? *Whoa.* Dad charges more than I thought for his tours. No wonder he didn't want to cancel tonight.

I board the bus last, glancing longingly at the empty seat

in the back. Back there, I could ignore everything Dad says and maybe even sneak in a little science project research on my cell phone. Just as I start moving toward it, Dad drops a hand to my shoulder and steers me toward a seat in the front.

"Up front, kiddo. You're my right-hand assistant tonight, and we can't communicate if we're on the opposite end of the bus!" With a wink, he adds, "Plus, this is your first time on the tour. Don't want you to miss any of the good stuff!"

Right. The good stuff.

Dad taps on the microphone attached to his headset. "Ladies and gentlemen, welcome to the Spirits of Chicago tour!"

A smattering of applause ripples through the bus. Dad grins and tips an imaginary hat, then climbs into the driver's seat. "I know you've all met my daughter, Claire. She'll be my assistant for the evening. Please let her know if you need anything."

I turn around and give an awkward wave as the bus lurches to life. Fishing my crumpled pamphlet out of my coat pocket, I skim the schedule. It's long.

Dad's voice pipes through the speakers again. "Our first stop is what many historians and ghost hunters refer to as the Alley of Death. In a moment, we'll be disembarking for a brief stop at this infamous site."

The bus slows to a crawl. The alley to our right is dark. *Really dark.*

Dad navigates the bus onto the side of the street and turns the hazards on. He climbs out of his seat and gestures to the alley. "In 1903, the Iroquois Theater opened and was advertised as being completely fireproof. Five weeks after the grand opening, a matinee performance of *Mr. Bluebeard* was onstage when a small fire started. That fire eventually spread through the entire theater, leading to the deaths of more than six hundred people."

He pauses for a moment to let that number sink in. Six hundred. That's a lot of death. I turn around and look at the sea of concerned faces behind me, then chuckle. Dad might be able to scare the adults on this bus with his ghost nonsense, but I've heard it all. He can't faze me.

"You see, the theater wasn't really built all that well. In an effort to save money, many of the safety features that would have made it fireproof were skipped. Instead of fire escapes, there were metal platforms with one-hundred-foot drops down to the cobblestone street. Instead of fireproof materials, there were wooden seats stuffed with hemp and a paper curtain on the stage. By the time the blaze started, there was nothing anyone could do. The theater lit up like a match."

Lit up like a match. I let my eyes flutter closed and imagine the thick black smoke billowing up into the Chicago sky. It sounds every bit as bad as the Great Chicago Fire. How could those builders have been so careless?

The door lets out a high-pitched whine as it slowly opens. Goose bumps break out on my arms.

Get a grip on yourself, Claire. He's not even talking about ghosts yet. And even if he starts, none of it is real. Sure, I used to think it was when I was little, but not anymore. I'm a scientist now. Scientists know better than to believe in things like ghosts.

Right?

Dad removes his headset. "You okay, Claire? You look a little pale."

I look out the door into the smear of blackness blanketing the alley. I know the stories about this alley are fake, but it feels different than I expected it to. Unsettling. "Yeah. Sorry. I just got a little motion sick on the way here."

Even in the dim overhead lighting, I can see his eyebrows crinkle together. "Are you going to throw up?"

"No. No, I'm good." I get to my feet and motion for the passengers behind me to go ahead. They file past me one at a time, their eyes trained on the inky alley. After the last person passes me, I settle the brim of my baseball cap down low over my eyes, then shuffle reluctantly toward the door.

"You don't have to stay on the bus. Just stick close enough to it that if a police officer shows up and wants it moved, you can motion to me. Okay?"

I nod in understanding and step into the icy night air. It still smells like spring, though—like damp soil and sprouting flowers. I head into the alley and wait for my eyes to adjust to the darkness. Once they do, I notice that framed posters hang on one side, and there are some large metal fire escapes dangling above us. Didn't they have those the day the fire broke out?

The group settles into a half-circle shape with Dad in the center. A woman in front of me raises her hand. Dad nods at her.

"I guess I'm still not sure why this is called the Alley of Death," she says. "I understand the fire happened next door, but what does that have to do with this alley?"

"Oh, didn't I tell you? The lucky folks who managed to reach the metal platforms were forced to jump to escape the flames. They landed right. About. There." Dad points to the ground beneath my feet. "*That's* how the alley got its name."

I fight off a shudder as I look down at the weathered pavement. This isn't how I imagined the stops on Dad's tour would be at all. I figured I'd be following him through a grave-yard while he popped out from behind gravestones to scare people or something. This is...I don't know, more sinister. More real.

I don't like it.

A man wearing a bright blue Cubs stocking cap raises

his hand next. He looks disturbed. "I read something about the fire years ago that said no one was ever prosecuted for what happened that day. Is that true?"

"Sadly, yes."

My mind snaps back to the party Mom hosted for Dad at a local bookstore when his novel came out. Dad gave a little speech before he cut the cake and signed books. I remember him saying that ghost legends often come from something called *unavenged* deaths, meaning deaths that shouldn't have happened but that no one ever paid the price for. If no one ended up on trial for the theater fire, then we really are standing in the exact spot where hundreds of unavenged deaths happened. More than six hundred, to be exact. The perfect fuel for the kind of ghost legend Dad loves to write about. No wonder this alley has such a scary name. It earned it.

My phone vibrates in my hand, startling me. It's the alarm for the five-minute warning. I wave my hand at Dad, letting him know it's nearly time to get back on the bus, then let my eyes sweep over the alley one final time. If I never see this place again, I'll be fine with that. Actually, I think I'll be grateful.

SIX

The next fifteen minutes are boring, since traffic is moving like a turtle and Dad is droning on about some disaster involving a boat called the SS *Eastland*. Apparently, it sank in the Chicago River right at the intersection of LaSalle Street and Wacker Drive. A lot of people drowned. I can't help but tune him out a little, because I've heard it all before. Thankfully, there's no good place to park the tour bus, so this part of the tour is just a drive-by.

"Our next stop is Hull-House," Dad says. "Hull-House was founded in 1889 as a settlement house for European immigrants. It was also the site of a supposedly haunted attic, a haunted garden, and a devil baby!"

I laugh to myself as he continues explaining, because really, how could anyone believe in a devil baby with red eyes? Nineteen thirteen must have been a wild time, because the rumor of a child with horns, scaly skin, and pointed ears apparently had *everyone* talking.

The bus slows down, and again the door creaks open with all the attitude of a cranky old man. Hull-House looms outside, all of the windows darkened. It's larger than I expected it to be.

"Should I just wait on the bus this time? Keep an eye out in case we need to move it?"

"Nah," Dad answers. "The traffic isn't as bad in this area; we park here all the time without problems."

I sigh, disappointed. Sitting in a warm bus sounded really nice.

"Ladies and gentlemen, feel free to roam around. Hull-House now functions as a museum, which is closed for the day, but you can still look through the windows and explore the grounds."

The passengers file past in a blur of excited chatter. I step off the bus, pausing to swap out my baseball cap for a thicker hat that covers my ears. I still don't want to be seen wandering around this place, but I'd rather not lose my ears to frostbite, either.

I'm just about to pull the door shut when I hear a muffled whisper coming from inside. Oh no—did I accidentally leave someone behind? I exhale a shaky breath, disappointed in myself. Dad said no one can ever be on the bus without one of us. *It's a liability*, he said. I promised I'd make sure that didn't happen. Maybe I'm not any better at this than Sam would've been after all.

My eyes travel up to the bus's darkened windows. Left to right, I scan each one for movement. Just when I'm beginning to think I imagined the whisper, a blur streaks past one of the rear windows, startling me.

Someone *is* on the bus! I clamber up the steps, hoping I can get them off and back on the tour before Dad notices. When I reach the top of the steps, I realize the little blue floor lights on either side of the aisle aren't lit up. They must turn off when the bus isn't running. Shards of moonlight break up the darkness, but it's still not enough for me to see who stayed behind.

"Hello?" I call out, my voice echoing down the rows of empty seats.

When no one answers, I start walking toward the back of the bus. I tell myself not to count, that I'm looking for a stubborn passenger and not one of Dad's ghouls, but I'm still shaky, so I give in and do it anyway.

One...

Two...

Three...

I check each row as I pass, frowning at the seats. Other than a few gum wrappers and some backpacks the passengers stowed away, they're empty. By the time I reach the last row, I'm shaking. Where did they go?

The wind suddenly gusts, creating an eerie howling sound as it passes through an open window. Leaning over a seat, I use both hands to gently close it, then latch the top. Could that have been what I heard? The wind? But even if the whispering sound was actually wind whistling through the bus, that still wouldn't explain what I saw.

I'm about to leave the bus when I remember there's a bathroom. I haven't seen it yet, but I noticed Dad put a line about it on the brochures. *The restroom is located at the rear of the bus.* I should check it, make sure someone isn't sick or doing something illegal, right? Dad once told me people have done weird things on his tour before, like trying to steal stuff from the stops to keep as memorabilia. But what would someone steal from a bus bathroom? Toilet paper? Hand soap?

I blink at the narrow door and tell myself to get it over with before Dad comes looking for me. Taking a few steps forward, I knock. A thump of movement from the other side makes me lurch backward.

"Is someone in there?" My voice comes out shaky.

I grip the handle. It's so cold I pull my hand back like I've been stung. Another thump echoes from inside. I go stiff, taking another step backward even though I know it's not what a real scientist would do. A real scientist would open the door and investigate. Then again, a real scientist wouldn't be on this bus to begin with.

"You waiting on that bathroom, hon?" A shrill voice from the other end of the bus makes me jump. It's Toga Woman. I press a hand to my chest and focus on breathing. She tilts her head to the side, probably trying to figure out why I'm hanging out on an empty bus.

"I...I think someone is in there." I stammer over my words, feeling stupid.

"Really? I didn't notice anyone missing outside." She shimmies down the narrow aisle between the seats and raps loudly on the bathroom door. "Nature calls out here, friend. Tinkle, tinkle, flush, flush!"

I'd laugh if I weren't so on edge. When no one answers her, she grips the handle and jerks the door open. I don't know what I expect to see, but a small, empty bathroom isn't it.

"Well. Guess that answers that question," she says. "I'll just be a minute. Too much coffee tonight." She waves a disposable cup in the air, laughing.

I wince and let out an uncomfortable *ha-ha*. Toga Woman

disappears inside the tiny bathroom, leaving me alone in the dark. Plopping down into the nearest seat, I exhale a shaky breath. This tour is already getting to me. I'm just as bad as Dad, scaring myself like that. As much as I'd like to run off this bus and never come back, I can't. Instead, I twiddle my fingers and look out the window at Hull-House. Its windows are dark. The yard is draped in shadows that shift with every gust of wind.

"Hey, kiddo." Dad suddenly appears at the bus door. His hair is sticking up from the wind, and he's finally decided to zip up his coat. "Whatcha doing in here?"

"Someone needed to use the bathroom, so I stayed behind so they weren't alone on the bus." I leave out the part about the shadow and the whispering and the thumps.

"Good thinking. As soon as they're finished"—Dad gestures to the pod of passengers posing for selfies on the front porch—"we can head out." He tips his head slightly, his eyebrows furrowing. "You okay? You look a little pale. Motion sick again?"

"Oh, um. Yeah," I answer, hoping Dad can't see the truth. I'm not pale because I'm motion sick. I'm pale because Toga Woman startled me and...well, maybe I am just a *little* scared. "I'll be fine, though. I'm already feeling better."

He gives me a cheerful thumbs-up. The bathroom door

swings open, and Toga Woman steps out. "Whew! Much better. Next time I go ghost hunting, I'll remember to get the tall latte instead of the grande!"

She and Dad laugh like this is the funniest thing in the world. Meanwhile, I'm wishing my seat would open up and swallow me. Anything to be done with this tour bus. I expected a miserable night, but this is more than that. I'll never admit it to Dad or anyone else, but the feeling deep down in my gut isn't just last night's burrito having a party. It's fear.

When everyone is settled back on the bus again, Dad announces that the next few stops will be drive-bys. We pass by the supposedly haunted Congress Hotel, wait for a sighting of the Woman in Red at the Drake, and then pass the spot where Dad *thinks* the real Resurrection Mary died. By the time he introduces our final stop, the other passengers are so excited that they're scream-talking over one another. It's deafening. I plug my ears and remind myself that my job is almost done.

"Our final stop is the Couch Tomb!" Dad croons into the screechy microphone. "Don't forget your cameras on the bus, guys. You're going to want pictures of this one."

Anxiety roils around in me. The first time I saw the Couch Tomb was when I was around nine years old. Mom took Sam and me to the park for a picnic. I didn't know it then, but the small stone building gaping at me with its dulled edges and black fencing was the last remaining grave site from when Lincoln Park used to be a city cemetery. It looked like a house, but instead of a door there was just a thick metal slab. No doorknob. No lock. No windows, either. Nothing but a word etched into the concrete above the door—COUCH.

Were people actually buried inside it? Why was it the only one there? What did COUCH mean? The questions pinging around in my nine-year-old head were endless. Little did I know that someday I'd be wandering around it in the dark.

The bus slows down again. The mausoleum is off in the distance, shrouded in shadows. The door slides open with a groan, and the passengers stampede past me, Dad right on their heels. They aren't just excited. They're manic.

It's official. These people have all lost their minds.

SEVEN

I give myself a mental pat on the back for wearing boots as our group trudges through the soggy grass toward the tomb. There are cars whooshing past the park on one side, and on the other side, the dark windows of the Chicago History Museum stare at us. It's strange to see a grave site sandwiched between all this other city stuff. Like the old *Sesame Street* game: *One of these things is not like the others.* Pretty sure even a two-year-old could pick this one out.

Dad waves for everyone to gather around. I stick to the back of the group, close enough to hear what he's saying but far enough that I can easily reach the bus if I need to. I triple-checked the seats *and* the bathroom this time, made 100 percent sure there wasn't anyone in there when I walked away.

"One oddity of this particular tomb is that we have no idea who is actually buried inside!" Camera flashes pop off in the dark. The rustle of a cough drop being unwrapped carries on the breeze. "There's a lot we still don't know about it. Not surprising, since no one has ever seen the inside."

I narrow my eyes at the building, confused. Why would the city of Chicago leave it here, right in plain sight, if they don't even know who is buried in it? It could be empty, for all they know. Empty and a total waste of space.

Dad catches my bewildered expression. "Have a question, Claire?"

My original goal was to avoid getting involved in this tour, but I can't. It's too hard. I guess when you're used to looking at things like a scientist, unanswered questions just aren't your friends.

Shrugging, I wave a hand at the squat structure. "I don't get why they don't move it or tear it down if it might be empty anyway." I look around the area, imagining how much nicer the view from the park would be if the tomb weren't there, always reminding people of death. "They took away all the other graves, you know?"

Even through the shadows, I can see a smile forming on my father's face. "Good question! While I can't answer for certain, my guess is that they don't remove it because it's history. Folks might not like the way it looks, but it represents a time of big change for Chicago."

O-kay. I can deal with that. I might even agree with it a little, though I'd probably never admit it. Dad once told me that he enjoys studying and writing about historical events because sometimes they get forgotten or told incorrectly over time. Like the Iroquois Theater fire. I've lived in Chicago my whole life and never heard of that! Sad, because so many people died in it.

I look back up at Dad, noticing that a familiar glint has formed in his eyes. I call it the ghost glint. It's how he looks when he's talking about something particularly sinister. I exhale a puff of disappointment, fully aware of what's coming next. Dad won't give a normal answer to this question. No, he's going to bring in ghosts.

"And if that isn't enough of a reason for the city to leave this tomb alone," he continues, "there's also the possibility of *complications* if they decide to move it."

"Complications?" Toga Woman asks. "You mean like permit issues or something?"

"No. *Restless spirits,*" Dad answers darkly. "You can't go moving final resting places without accepting the consequences, no matter how grim they may be."

"Ahhh...angry ghosts," Toga Woman whispers.

"Exactly." Dad crouches down and runs his hand over

the grass. "We already have plenty of restless spirits roaming Lincoln Park, if you consider that this land used to be a giant, sprawling cemetery."

Just as the word *cemetery* leaves his mouth, the wind picks up. It ruffles my hair and sends a parade of goose bumps up and down my bare neck. I take a steadying breath and remind myself it has nothing to do with what Dad is saying. There are no "restless spirits" here—just an old abandoned building that might as well be turned into a gardening shed. Dad is simply doing what he loves to do: scaring people.

I remember how things used to be. Back before Dad had the Spirits bus and a bunch of people who wanted to hear his ghost stories, he used to tell them all to Sam and me. Sometimes those stories were scary enough to keep me up at night for hours. Now that I'm twelve, I thought I was past all that. I thought I was brave. I was wrong.

"When it was decided that the cemetery would be moved, the workers didn't do a very good job. They dug up and relocated thousands of bodies, but they were sloppy and didn't keep good records as they worked. Then the Great Chicago Fire came through and destroyed the gravestones that were left. With nothing but piles of charred and sometimes completely shattered headstones, the city no longer knew who had been buried there to begin with."

A chill slides up my spine. Annoyed, I briskly rub the back of my neck to ward off the goose bumps.

An older man lifts his hand. "How did they figure it out?"

"They didn't," Dad answers matter-of-factly. "There are still around ten thousand bodies buried right here beneath our feet."

Ten thousand bodies? I look down, horrified.

"We have no idea who those poor souls were. All we know is that every time a new construction site is dug up for a parking lot or a house...skeletons surface." Dad taps on the ground one final time, then rises to a standing position. Meanwhile, I feel faint. I've been in graveyards before, so it isn't the idea of being close to dead people that's freaking me out. It's the fact that they're sprinkled around my entire neighborhood. All the places I love may be picture-perfect on the surface, but down below, it's another story. A grisly one.

My heart races as I shift my weight from one foot to the other. Who is buried directly beneath me right now? The question makes me light-headed all over again.

Sneaking a look at my cell phone, a rush of gratitude fills me. It's five-minute-warning time. I desperately point at my screen until Dad nods that he's gotten the hint.

I am *so* ready to get out of here.

"Ladies and gentlemen, I'm afraid our time together is coming to an end. Please take any last pictures of the mausoleum and return to the bus."

He doesn't have to tell me twice. My fingers and toes are numb, and my nerves are frayed. The bus door opens back up with a groan, and I clamber aboard first. I've just hit the top step and turned toward my seat when I see something that makes my breath catch in my throat. A little boy. He's sitting in the back row, looking down.

Where did he come from?

"Claire, honey, sit down. People are trying to get by, and you're blocking the aisle," Dad urges, just as someone bumps into me from behind.

I slide into my seat as fast as I can, then turn around and strain for a glimpse of the child. He's there, but even with the bus exploding into movement from all directions, he's still staring at the floor. He's got dark hair and is wearing some kind of old-fashioned-looking white suit. My eyes travel down as I notice that one of his small legs is angled into the aisle. His suit pants are too short, and his shoes are black.

My brain spins as I stare at him. I didn't see that boy when I searched the bus at Hull-House, and just ten minutes ago, I searched the bus again here at the mausoleum.

A tap on my shoulder pulls me from my thoughts.

"You okay? You look like you've seen a ghost," Dad says with a familiar chuckle.

"Mm-hmm." It's all I can say right now. Is that water dripping from the boy's head? It's not even raining outside...

Bodies shuffle as people continue to board, blocking my view of him for a minute. I lean way too far into the aisle, this time losing my balance and tumbling to the dirty floor.

"Claire!" Dad hisses. His voice is sharp this time.

I scramble up. There's something sticky on my palm. I don't even want to think about what that could be. "Yes?"

He glances toward the rear of the bus, then back to me. "I asked if you are okay, and you barely responded to me. Then you fall out of your seat? What are you looking at?"

"Nothing. Sorry, I just spaced out for a minute." I jam my sticky hand into my pocket and tell myself I'm done with the boy. In fact, the tour is over. I'm done with all of this.

"If you say so. Look, you've only got to hold yourself together for another twenty minutes or so, okay?" He slips his headset on and watches me for a response.

"Yeah. I mean, I'm good," I answer quietly. "Anything I need to do on the way back?"

"You could hand out the coupons from the bookstore."

"They already have them. I stuffed them in the brochures so I didn't have to hand things out twice."

Dad starts up the engine and buckles his seat belt. "Good thinking. I'll chat about my book a little on the way back, and hopefully some of them will look it up when they get home."

As the conversations around us grow quieter, I can't shake the feeling that something is wrong. *Missing.* I unzip my pockets and check for my phone. It's there. The big orange envelope with receipts in it is still sitting beside me on the seat. If something is missing, it isn't mine. Still, the feeling is eerie. It seeps through my skin and settles into my bones. I don't like it.

"Do you have everything you came here with?" I whisper to Dad. It makes no sense that he could have lost something on the tour tonight and I'd know about it before him, but nothing about this feeling makes sense.

He takes a hand off the steering wheel long enough to point at the small holder to the right of the driver's seat. Inside, I can see his house keys, his money clip, a flashlight, a pen, and a few balls of lint. "I think so. Why?"

I shrug. It's impossible to explain this feeling to him, so I don't try. I can explain fear. I can explain sadness. I can explain anger. In fact, I'm pretty sure I've felt all three in the past twenty-four hours! But this feeling...it's different. *Bad.* Like a little crack has started way down in the center of me, and it's growing wider. And for whatever reason, I'm starting to think it has something to do with the little boy.

Loosening my seat belt, I lean out into the aisle. The boy is sitting in the same spot, but this time his fearful eyes are not fixed on the ground anymore. They're focused on me. In the dim overhead lighting, they look dark, almost black. His skin is pale, and his lips are turned down.

The boy mouths something to me, but no matter how hard I squint, I can't figure out what it is. His lips are moving too fast. Best I can tell, he's saying three different words.

Want, oh, the.

White, on, this.

Were, are, that.

It makes no sense. The bad feeling inside me sprouts thick black roots. I don't know if the boy is sick or in danger, but as soon as this bus stops, I've got to figure out what he's trying to tell me.

The bus jerks across a lane of traffic, and I fumble for something to hold on to. When it finally chugs to a stop, I gather my bag and stand up on shaky legs. It's time to get some answers.

"I'm happy to stick around for a few minutes to answer any questions about future tours or my book," Dad says into the microphone, startling me. Has he been talking this entire time?

"Can I sit on the bus for a minute while the passengers get off? I need to see something," I ask in a shaky voice.

"Haven't you seen enough for tonight?" Dad says with a laugh, removing his headset and hanging it over the steering wheel. "I need you to peel the logos off the bus and get them rolled back up."

He starts moving toward the door, and I tug on his sleeve. "*Please*. Just let everyone else get off first, and then I promise I'll go get the logos."

A frown settles on his face. "You're supposed to be helping me, Claire, not hiding on this bus."

"I'm sorry. I'm just..." *Worried*. The dark eyes of that little boy are haunting me, and I need to make sure he leaves with someone. If nothing else, he's gotta get to a doctor about that pale skin. My mind veers off, landing on an even scarier thought. What if he was trying to tell me he's been kidnapped? That would be horrible! What would I do?

Wait. Kidnapped by who? Lens Cap Guy? Toga Woman? No way. And why would someone who kidnapped a kid take him on a tour bus, anyway?

Worst hypothesis ever, Claire.

Whatever. The most important thing is that I make sure he's okay before Dad and I go home.

Dad sighs at my silence. "Fine. Two minutes. But please make sure you're still available to passengers who have questions."

I nod a silent thank-you to him. The group files past me one at a time until the bus is empty. I sneak a peek at the back row.

He's gone. The little boy is just...*gone.*

EIGHT

I rub my eyes with the heels of my hands to clear my vision. I watched every last person file off this bus, and the little boy was not one of them. He wasn't with a parent, a grandparent, or a friend, and he wasn't alone. *He. Wasn't. There.*

"Seriously? Where is he?" I head toward the back of the bus. The bad feeling is stuck in me now, climbing my insides like those annoying vines that cover our building.

Dad peeks back in the bus door and meets my eyes. "Claire? What are you looking for now?"

"The little boy. Where is the little boy who was back here?"

He looks puzzled. "There weren't any children on the tour tonight. I don't allow anyone under the age of twelve."

I shake my head, bewildered. No way was that boy older

than twelve. He was six, seven tops. Weaving my way down the aisle, I stop at the seat the boy was sitting in. It's damp. There's a crumpled piece of paper on the floor that also looks wet. Snatching it up, I carefully uncurl its edges. My hands are shaking so hard I can barely get the fragile paper open enough to read it.

When I finally get the paper flattened, I stare at it numbly. It's blank except for the number 396 scrawled in the center. Other than the fact that there's a hole in the bottom and that it looks kind of old and faded, there isn't much in the way of clues.

I look back up into my father's face. "You are *sure* you didn't see a little boy sitting back here? Brown hair, white suit?"

"I didn't. Sorry." Dad lifts an eyebrow. "Are you telling me *you* saw a little boy sitting here just now?"

There's a hint of hope in his voice. Of course, there is. If I say I saw a little boy sitting here and then he vanished, Dad can twist that all up into another one of his dumb ghost stories and use it to sell more tickets. He might even write it into a book. Before I know it, he'll make our house a stop on one of his tours. We'll be talked about more than we already are. No thank you.

"No. I didn't see anything." My stomach lurches as the lie leaves my lips. The little boy was here; I saw him with my own eyes. Folding the paper in half, I carefully stick it in my jeans pocket. It's probably nothing more than the tag from a dry-cleaning service or valet. But I keep it anyway. I keep it because I can't get rid of the thought that the wet boy with dark eyes left it for me.

~~~

Most nights, I fall asleep as soon as my head hits the pillow. I blame it on seventh grade. You can't expect a girl to sit through things like Spanish, pre-algebra, and history without getting exhausted. It's impossible.

But tonight is different. Tonight, I'm lying in bed, thinking about the boy on the bus. His face was so pale. And those dark eyes... I'm half-afraid I'll never forget them and half-afraid I will. What was he mouthing to me, anyway? No matter how many times I run that moment through my brain, I can't make sense of the words.

And then he was gone. Vanished right into thin air like he was never there to begin with. Only I know he was.

White face. Pale lips. Dark eyes. Number 396. A million thoughts crash around in my mind as I stare up at the ceiling. It has more cracks in it tonight than I remember. Dark ones. Jagged veins snake their way across the white paint and stop where the walls meet the ceiling. It kinda reminds me of an ant farm. I always hated them, thought it was bananas to bring *any* bugs into the house on purpose, but Sam loved them. Pretty sure he named every one of the little black nasties Claire just to upset me.

I'm trying to drift off to sleep when a faint scratching sound starts up in the wall behind my head. *Scritch scratch. Scritch scratch. Scritch scratch.* My heart gallops around in my chest. I listen, swallowing hard when the scratching gets louder. I've never heard this before, not once in the twelve years I've lived in this place. Maybe it's a mouse? I pull my blankets tighter around my neck and try to ignore it. *It's nothing scary. It's nothing scary. It's nothing sca—*

Scriiiiiiiitch scraaaaaaaaaaaatch.

The scratching is drawn out this time, like nails slowly dragging down a chalkboard. I focus on the beams of light coming through my window from the street, wishing they were brighter so they could light up my room. Better yet, I wish that I were brave enough to just reach over and turn on my lamp. Instead, I'm frozen in place, and my entire room is blanketed in a deep, terrifying darkness.

It must be a mouse. I try to imagine him in there—his little whiskers and curled-up tail—and tell myself he's cute. Not something big and hairy and fanged trying to get into my room. Just a hungry little mouse looking for some crumbs. He'll eat and then leave, and I'll never hear him again.

Only I do.

The scratching grows more frantic, and now I can hear little bits of plaster inside my wall breaking off and falling. If I didn't know better, I'd think someone was trying to claw their way out of the wall and into my bed.

I immediately start counting. *One...two... three...* The only thing keeping me from screaming my head off is the calm that counting brings me. *Four...five...six...* Think about happy things, Claire. Puppies. Rainbows. Ice cream. I start sweating despite the chill in my room.

The scratching stops for a moment, leaving me in the most dreadful quiet I've ever heard. Whoever came up with the phrase "silence is golden" was a moron. It's awful. I'm poised to climb out of bed and race down to the living room to sleep on the sofa when the doorknob starts rattling. My blood runs cold.

Mice can't rattle doorknobs.

The rattling stops for a minute, then starts back up, harder than before. I choke back a sob. My door doesn't even have a lock on it, so that means whoever or *whatever* is on the other side is just trying to scare me. But why? A thousand terrible possibilities flicker through my mind.

"Sam? Is that you? You stop it right now if it is!" I hiss into the darkness.

I wait for an answer, but I get nothing. No scratching. No

rattling. No Sam. Just the painful beating of my own heart in my ears.

My curtains suddenly billow out as if they are caught in a breeze. They look like two pale yellow ghosts bouncing around the pane of glass. I stare in horror at my window, remembering that I double-checked the lock on it before I climbed into bed. It's secured tightly. Fluttering curtains when there's no breeze can only mean one thing: There's something in my room, and it isn't a mouse.

I've got to get out of here.

Scrambling out of bed, I trip over my backpack and crash to the hardwood floor. Pain shoots up my tailbone as I drag myself to the nightstand. I fumble around for the pull cord on my lamp. I think I'm screaming, but I can't tell because the scratching has started up again, and it's loud. So loud I cover my ears and curl up into a ball on the floor. The bad feeling from the bus rushes back. Something is missing. Something is missing.

Something is missing.

My door bursts open, and light from the hallway floods my room. It isn't the boy from the bus, though—it's Mom. "Claire! What's wrong? Are you okay?"

I'm shaking so hard I can barely answer her. I sit up and squeak out a feeble "yes."

The cracks in my ceiling look normal now, nothing more than thin hairline breaks in the paint. The scratching has stopped.

Mom looks terrified. Her eyes are wide, startled. One side of her hair is pointing skyward. "Honey, talk to me. Did you have a bad dream?"

I wish it were only a bad dream. But something tells me it wasn't. Shaking my head, I swipe at the tears on my cheeks. It wasn't a mouse scratching inside my wall. It wasn't Sam trying to scare me. And it wasn't my imagination.

It was the boy from the bus.

The thought worms its way into my brain, scaring me even more. It's scary because it isn't logical. I have no evidence that the boy I saw on the bus has anything to do with what just happened.

Do I?

I think back to the moment the boy first appeared. Even though he was dripping wet, wearing weird clothes, and sick looking, no one else on the bus seemed to notice him. The woman sitting in the seat directly across from him acted like he wasn't there! Then there's the fact that he didn't try to communicate with anyone but me. If he were a lost kid, wouldn't he have asked one of the adults for help? It just doesn't add up.

Unless...

Unless the little boy wasn't a lost child at all. My mind sifts through the few facts I know as if I've just completed a science experiment. Usually there's one hypothesis that makes more sense than the others. Unfortunately, in this case the hypothesis that keeps popping into my brain is one of the most ridiculous thoughts I've ever had. It's also one of the scariest.

"Claire?" Mom presses.

I snap back to the present. "I'm sorry. I just heard some weird stuff. I got scared."

Mom's forehead scrunches up into a mess of worried lines. "Like what?"

"Scratching," I answer. "And my doorknob was rattling."

She glances at the window. The wind is lashing a limb from our huge oak tree against the glass. It looks like a gnarled claw thrashing in the shadows.

"It's windy out there tonight. Looks like we're going to get a storm. You probably heard your window rattling, sweetie."

With this, she helps me to my feet and pulls me into a hug. I know I shouldn't need this. I mean, I'm in seventh grade. But *still*. The feeling lodged in the pit of my stomach is horrible.

"Get some sleep, okay? You had a big night, and you're probably overstimulated."

I look away from her, too upset to make eye contact. The sound I heard wasn't a storm or my window. It was my doorknob rattling. No matter how much I want there to be a rational, *scientific* explanation for what just happened, there isn't.

Promising Mom that I'm okay, I finally manage to shoo her out of my room. Once the door is firmly closed, I sink down to the floor and blow out a shaky breath. No matter how many different ways I analyze the data, my theory ends up the same: The little boy on the bus was not *just* a little boy.

My hands shake as I clasp them together in my lap. Sweat beads at my hairline. The word I keep trying to force out of my brain refuses to leave. Over and over it surfaces until I finally allow myself to listen. To consider it.

Ghost.

What if a ghost followed me home?

NINE

I slept in my closet last night because I was too much of a chicken to sleep in my bed but too afraid to walk down our creaky old stairwell to the living room in the dark, either. The small space covered in dirty clothes and mismatched socks seemed like a good compromise, so I carried my quilt and pillow in there. With a flashlight and an old Louisville Slugger at my side, I finally drifted off to sleep.

I have no idea how I'll sleep tonight.

Dragging my bedding out of the closet, I toss it into a pile on my mattress. I smooth it down as much as possible, hoping the bed looks freshly slept in. I don't want Mom and Dad to know where I slept last night. They'd ask questions, questions that I'd have to lie to answer.

Glancing around, I force myself to remember how things looked last night. The cracks in my ceiling. The curtains that danced around my window even though there was no wind to move them. The scratching in the walls. My room has never looked or felt like that before. Rubbing at my tired eyes, I think back to what Mom said. *Overstimulated.* I guess I do get like that sometimes, but usually it's about science stuff, not scratching sounds in the walls and terrible, unexplainable feelings.

No. Last night wasn't all me. It couldn't have been, because even now, with the sunlight spilling through the window, things still don't seem right. I feel like I'm being watched. A sharp pang of fear rockets through me.

Ghost.

The word pops back into my head even though I try to block it out. Not even twenty-four hours ago, I laughed and rolled my eyes at every ghost-related thing Dad said. I told myself his "spirits" were no more real than the haunted houses Sam and I go to every Halloween. Now? I'm shaking like a leaf in my own bedroom and beginning to wonder if everything I've ever believed is false. Not good. Not good at all.

Glancing down at the screen of my cell phone, I blow out a puff of disappointment. Still no texts from Casley. Maybe I should text her? She is still my best friend, after all. I start a message three different times before giving up. Texting Casley now, when she's obviously busy with Emily, will only make me look desperate.

I drag myself downstairs. The smell of something sweet hits me the second I clear the kitchen door. The light is on in the oven, and I can just barely see something puffing up inside a baking pan.

"Hungry, kiddo?"

Startling away from the oven window, I bump my head on the handle. I rub at the tender spot on my scalp. "Not really."

Totally untrue. I'm starving. Whatever Mom is baking smells incredible, but I'm still mad that she and Dad made me go on that ghost tour.

Mom swipes her finger across the screen of her iPad. Then she turns it around so I can look at the recipe. "They're homemade cinnamon rolls. I just made cream cheese frosting for them. You *sure* you're not hungry?"

My mouth waters. Cinnamon rolls with cream cheese frosting? If anything can test my willpower, it's the combination of ooey-gooey cinnamon and cream cheese. Just one taste wouldn't be bad, right?

She grabs a wooden spoon from the bowl next to the sink. It's coated with frosting. "I saved this for you. If you want it, that is."

Snatching the spoon before I can change my mind, I jam it in my mouth. It's perfect.

I finish licking the spoon just as Dad opens the back

door. He's wearing a black leather jacket with the Spirits of Chicago logo emblazoned across the back. His thinning salt-and-pepper hair is slicked back like that of some kind of greasy detective, and the T-shirt peeking out from underneath his jacket features a graveyard blanketed in mist.

"Morning! How did you sleep?"

I didn't.

"Fine," I answer, setting the spoon down. Just thinking about what happened in my room last night makes my heart speed up and my appetite go away.

"Good. Thanks again for the help on the bus last night. You were great!" He elbows me with a grin. "I told Josh that he'd better watch his back, or you might just take over for him someday."

He means this as a compliment, but it still makes me uneasy. Take over for Joshua? Nope. I'm not going back on that bus. Ever.

"Oh!" Mom exclaims. "I know you're eager to work on your science fair project, but could you do me one quick favor?"

"Sure. What?"

"Could you help your father with the trash? He's already carried down two loads, and I don't want him to aggravate his back again."

Dad tries to wave her off, but Mom shakes her head. "No.

Don't argue about this, David. You know how your back is. Let Claire help, please."

"I can do it," I say, trudging toward the back door. I'm exhausted, and carrying trash down the back stairs doesn't sound fun, but I have no choice. Dad's back acts up all the time, and if it gets really bad, he can't even get out of bed. I point to the black garbage bags sitting next to the door. "Just these two?"

"Yup. Thanks, Claire," Dad says, easing down into a chair.

I huff and puff to the bottom of our steps, stopping abruptly. Oh no. The big trash bins aren't in our backyard anymore. Dad said they were taking up too much room, so he moved them into the alley. I completely forgot. Now I'll have to go in there again. *Alone.* I look up at the gray sky, frowning. Just my luck. No sunshine.

Slinging a bag over each of my shoulders, I plod to the mouth of the alley. The first two bins look full, so that means I'll need to walk to the last one. The farthest one. I take a few steps in. The familiar smell of rotting food wafts by, making me gag. Just as I reach the third bin, a blast of icy air hits me in the face.

I'm still catching my breath when something begins scraping against the brick wall to my left. My imagination runs wild. It could be a pigeon, or it could be a giant rat. Or it could be something *much* worse. It could be the thing that was in my room last night. The sound stops, only to start up again immediately in another area of the alley.

My hands clench into fists as the scraping pauses, then begins again. It's to my right this time. Close. Too close. The trash bags slip from my shoulders and fall into a heap on the ground. One bursts open, peppering the cement with eggshells and splotches of flour.

Just then, something darts across the alley—a dark and shapeless something. It skitters behind a recycling bin and disappears. I shriek and stumble backward, tripping over the bags I dropped. Barely catching myself before I hit the ground, I spin around and sprint toward the exit.

One...

Two...

Three...

I can still hear the scraping behind me, like sharpened nails against brick. It sounds like it's drawing closer. Chasing me. When I reach the mouth of the alley, I gather the courage to sneak a look over my shoulder. The scraping stops. Other than our broken trash bags strewn across the cement, everything looks normal. I'd like to believe my eyes, but the little voice inside me says not to. Things haven't been normal since I stepped foot on Dad's tour bus, and this proves it. I've always hated this alley, but nothing bad has ever happened to me here. Not until now.

I'm gonna need a new front door key. Fast.

TEN

Monday rears its ugly head even though I only got about five hours of sleep the whole weekend. Definitely not enough to survive. I've been sitting on the edge of my bed for ten minutes, rubbing my tired eyes and trying to move.

Get it together, Claire. You need clothes ASAP, or you're going to be late for school, I tell myself. My body feels heavy as I pad across my chilly floor. I pick through a few piles of clothes, deciding to wear a mostly clean pair of jeans and a sweatshirt. Everything else lying around smells like it either needs to be washed or burned, so I head for the dresser to grab socks. I gasp as my hand makes contact with the knob. It's freezing. And wet! I cautiously kneel down to take a closer look. The wood is slick, like something got spilled down the front of it. But what? Ever since I set a can of soda on the dresser last summer and it left a permanent ring on the wood, I don't even bring drinks in here.

Peering beneath the dresser, I notice a puddle underneath. Dread needles me. I tug on the knobs of the top drawer, grunting when it doesn't slide out easily. What's going on?

I plant my feet firmly on the ground, grab both knobs on the drawer, and lean backward to use my body weight. With a sharp crack, it finally comes loose. Something cold sloshes out onto my floor and my bare feet. Water. It's puddled in the bottom of the drawer, and all my clothes are drenched.

"Holy cats, what in the—" I stop myself, afraid that if I get too loud, Mom will come barreling in. Or worse, Dad. I have no way to explain this, and even though I hate to admit it, Dad would be thrilled. My poor, wet wardrobe would be just one more "weird happening" for him to research so he could use it in a book.

With shaking hands, I work at the drawer until I get it shut again. Taking a step back, I look up at the ceiling for any sign of a leak. Nothing. Not even a water spot or yellowed area in the paint. It doesn't make sense, but I can't deal with this now, or I'll be late for school. I yank the sweatshirt and jeans on, then run a brush through my hair and pull it back. With everything in my dresser dripping wet, I'll have to borrow socks from Mom.

By the time I walk out the front door, I'm ten minutes

behind schedule. Today is gonna stink. Instead of figuring out why I suddenly have a swamp in my bedroom instead of a dresser full of clean clothes, I'll be at school. Every time I think I've calmed down, I remember the water splashing out onto my feet and get scared all over again.

I drag myself down the street, trying to focus on the signs of spring around me. The morning is crisp, and the trees have all sprouted little buds. By next month, they'll be full leaves, and my neighborhood will be green again. It's like magic, really. One minute Chicago is freezing and blanketed in snow, and the next it's a palette of different hues. Yellow daffodils. Lavender lilacs. Pink tulips. I can't wait.

As the doors of my school come into view, I remind myself that today is going to be better than my morning was. No bad feelings. No creepy sounds or fluttering curtains. No swamp dresser. Nothing but—

"Hey, Claire!" A voice carries on the stiff breeze.

It's Casley. She's barreling toward me with a huge grin on her face. Normally I'd run to her, maybe even pull her into a giant bear hug, but today feels different. Like there's an invisible wall between us.

She stops just short of me. Her cheeks are flushed pink, and she's breathless, probably from speed-walking here like she always does.

"How was your weekend?"

"Great," I lie. She was probably watching movies and eating popcorn with Emily while I was trying to survive Dad's ghost tour. Why didn't she invite me? Or at least text me about it? I wouldn't have felt half as left out if she'd *tried* to include me.

Cas quirks up an eyebrow. "Really? Because Sam said something to Chris about you going on your dad's tour bus. I didn't think you'd be caught dead on that thing!"

"Since when did you start listening to my brother about anything?" I ask with a laugh. I mean for it to sound joking, but it comes out wrong. Fake.

Something flickers in Casley's expression, and she rolls her shoulders. "Just seemed like a weird thing to make up."

"Yeah, well, remember when he told everyone he had a girlfriend last year? *Lola?*" I snort.

Casley's shoulders shake with laughter, sending a swath of blond hair into her eyes. She brushes it away quickly, gasping to catch her breath between giggles. "Yes! He kept telling us she went to another school and they met at hockey camp."

His so-called girlfriend always sounded a bit suspect to us, and it turned out we were right to be suspicious. Lola wasn't even a person! It was just the brand name on my favorite face mask. Sam stole the name and made up an entire story about a beautiful Swedish exchange student at a different school who fell in love with him.

"Well, good ol' Lola did teach us something, at least," I say.

"What's that?"

"That Sam has good taste in face masks!" I can't help the giggle that bubbles out of me this time. Casley joins in, her deep belly laugh carrying on the breeze.

It's moments like these when I remember why we've been best friends since second grade. Cas is comfortable. Like an old pair of slippers, or the baggy sweatshirt you want to sleep in when you're sick. I never thought anything would come between us.

Casley finally stops laughing. She tosses me a smile. "For the record, I didn't believe Sam, anyway. I know how much you hate that bus. I figured if your dad had forced you to go on it, you'd have called me."

I would have, if you hadn't ditched me.

My spirits plummet all over again. The words I want to say to Casley are on the tip of my tongue—that I wish things could go back to the way they were last year, when it was just her and me and the science club. Everything was so much simpler then, back before Emily and the ghost bus and the little boy with dark eyes. But I can't tell her all of that. Not now. Maybe not ever.

I need to change the subject.

Pointing at the cosmetics bag in her hand, I ask probably the dumbest question ever. "What is that, anyway?"

"Oh!" Casley's hazel eyes light up. "It's a makeup bag! Emily's mom used to work at some fancy cosmetics store in New York, so she knows all these cool makeup tips and tricks. Today she's bringing some makeup samples and—"

And I've heard enough. I have to borrow socks to wear because my dresser is flooded, and Casley is bragging about her new bestie? Besides, wasn't it like last week that Casley said makeup was totally overrated?

"Cool. Um, I just forgot I have an early meeting with my adviser," I say, cutting her off. "I better go."

Casley's face is pained. "Oh, okay. See you at lunch?"

"Sure," I answer, but I don't mean it. Emily will sit at our table for sure, and I'll be the odd one out. *Again*. No matter how much I try to participate in the conversations, it never works. They'll laugh at inside jokes, talk about makeup I've never even heard of, and spend more time gossiping about the cute boys in our grade than eating their lunches. I'd have more fun hanging out with the soccer team girls, and I don't even play soccer!

With a wave, I turn and walk away before she can see the tears welling in my eyes. Back in September, I thought this was going to be the best year ever. Casley and I had big plans! We were going to team up and win the science fair together. We were going to go to the seventh-grade dance together so neither of us would need to worry about asking a boy. We were going to buy that microscope. Now, thanks to her new friendship with Emily, Casley hasn't mentioned any of that stuff in a long time.

Yeah, if I had any thoughts of telling her about what happened to me this weekend, they're gone now. The old Casley would have understood. She would've helped me. The new Casley? She's probably too busy to even listen.

ELEVEN

First, second, and third periods are extra painful today. I check the clock so many times during Spanish that Señorita Jennings gives me a nasty look and asks me if I have somewhere better to be. At least I think that's what she asks. I'm not that good at Spanish.

I'm just getting in the hot lunch line when Cas catches up with me again. We don't have any morning classes together because she's in a different section, so I haven't seen her since before school. She sets her tray down on the metal rail and taps my shoulder until I look up.

My gaze lifts to find rosy cheeks, bubblegum lips, and perfect porcelain skin. Metallic pink eye shadow is brushed across her eyelids, and a few tendrils of blond hair frame her face.

"Well? Do you like it?" she asks, spinning in a quick circle.

I'm stunned into silence. Casley doesn't just look

different; she looks older. More mature. How did she change so much since the last time I saw her? This morning, her hair was wild, falling into her face every time she laughed. Now it's shiny and smooth with just enough curl to look elegant. And her clothes? Also perfect. Washed-out jeans, a faux fur vest, and the most adorable brown boots I've ever seen. I don't know how she managed this in between classes, but Casley looks like a model.

"Claire?" she says, her eyebrows cinching together in worry. "You're looking at me like I just fell out of a spaceship onto your front lawn!"

"Sorry," I mumble, my eyes snapping back down to the empty tray I'm holding. "I was just surprised."

"Good surprised, or *get to a bathroom and wash everything off* surprised?"

It's not hard to catch the hope in Casley's voice. "You look good, Cas. Are those your clothes? I've never seen them."

She fingers the vest, sighing wistfully. "I wish. They're Emily's. She brought them today for me to try on. Back before she moved here, she had a subscription to one of those clothes services that sends you different outfits every month. Guess you can keep what you want and send back what you don't like. I'm thinking of trying it out."

"Really?"

Her face sours like she just bit into a lemon. "Yeah, why? You think it's a bad idea?"

I shrug. "Just doesn't seem like something you'd be into. Renting clothes, I mean."

Casley goes silent for a moment. She brushes an invisible speck off the front of the fur vest, her lips slightly turned down. "Yeah. Maybe. I don't know."

Casley shoves her tray closer to mine, grimacing at the options behind the steamed-up glass. Her wrist is covered in dangly silver bracelets. I wonder if she borrowed those from Emily, too.

"Ugh. Why didn't I bring a lunch today?" she moans. "I think I'm going to just grab something from the salad bar. Meet me at the table, 'kay?"

I can't help but notice a table of eighth-grade boys watching as she crosses the cafeteria and stops at the salad bar. She's one of the prettiest girls in the school, and now that she's getting makeovers from the cute new girl, she's going to be one of the most popular.

And me? Sam once told me that if I were an animal instead of a human, I'd be a mouse. Some people might think mice are cute and that this was a compliment. I know it wasn't, though, and every time I look at my pointy little nose, I remember it.

Someone bumps into me from behind, sending my

orange off the edge of my tray and onto the floor. I spin around to see who it was but only catch a glimpse of a boy pushing through the lunch line in the opposite direction. Dark, wet hair. White suit. I gasp and stand on my tiptoes to see over the crowd. That couldn't be who I think it is, right?

"Lose this?"

I know that voice. My eyes snap to his face, confirming my suspicion. Warner Jameson. Captain of the baseball team. President of the robotics club. Owner of the perfect gray eyes.

The tips of my ears start burning as I take the orange from his hand. "Um, thanks."

"No problem." He scrunches his eyebrows together. "Everything okay?"

I turn around and scan the area again, noticing that the lunch line has thinned out, and there's no sign of the boy. Just like on the bus, though, I saw him. I know I did. "Yeah. I'm just clumsy."

"Me too," he says, pointing at the small red stain on his shirt. "Ketchup. Tater tot day is dangerous for me."

I laugh before I can stop myself. I point down at the puddle of yellowish gravy on my mashed potatoes. "Guess I'm living on the edge, too."

He lets out a loud guffaw and splits his stack of napkins in half, then places half of them on my tray. "You might need these, then."

"For sure. Ah, thanks for this." I wave my orange around in the air awkwardly.

Seriously, Claire?

Warner grins, and his dimples flash at me. "Cool. Catch you later, Claire."

Walking away, I can't keep the grin off my face. *I just talked to Warner Jameson.* I wish I could tell Casley about it, even if it was only like three sentences, but I'm afraid to. What would happen if she told Emily what I said? Would she laugh? Tell Warner?! I think about all the times I've seen Warner and Emily talking in the hallway or getting out of the same car in the morning and cringe. They're friends.

No. It's too risky. The conversation with Warner needs to stay a secret. I used to tell Casley all my secrets, even the most embarrassing ones. Now I can't tell her anything. Not about the conversation with Warner, and definitely not about how I'm not just *hearing* spooky things but *seeing* spooky things now, too. I didn't drop that orange on my own, just like I didn't fill my dresser drawers with water. The boy shoved me. The boy who looked a lot like the one who vanished from the bus.

I'm so overwhelmed. The thought of dealing with all this on my own makes my heart feel like it's being put through a paper shredder. Slowly.

"Claire?" Casley snags my sleeve as I'm about to walk by. Her face is pinched with worry. "You okay?"

"Yeah, fine. Why?"

"Maybe because you're frowning. Big-time."

You would frown too if there were a ghost in your house. I cringe at the thought I just allowed into my head again. What is wrong with me? I'm a scientist! I need to see evidence of something before I believe in it, and up until recently, there's never been any evidence solid enough to make me believe in ghosts.

There have been a lot of strange happenings, though. The scratching, the whispers, the rattling doorknob and flooded dresser. And the paper left on the bus seat, the one with 396 on it. Is that stuff proof enough that a ghost followed me home from the bus?

Maybe.

Balancing my tray on one arm, I rub my eyes for the millionth time, wincing at the burn that follows. I'm *so* tired. Everything is harder than usual, and I can't focus on anything. Normally, my thoughts run in nice straight lines, but today they're zigzagging all over the place.

"You're sitting here, right?" Casley pats the bench next to her expectantly. From directly across the table, Emily is watching. Waiting. Probably hoping I'll move on. "Please?"

"Oh, um..." I start, unsure of how to answer her. If I say yes, then I'm trapped. I'll have to sit through another unbearable lunch with Emily. But if I say no, I'll be pushing Casley even further away than she already is. Since I could use a friend right now, I sit.

Casley leans over and playfully bumps my shoulder with hers. For a moment, I feel better. Like I made the right choice. Then I notice the look on Emily's face. She's smiling, but it doesn't quite reach her eyes.

A loud crash echoes harshly off the cafeteria walls, startling me. I nervously stand up and look around, convinced I'm going to see those terrifying dark eyes fixed on me all over again. Instead, I see a mess of mashed potatoes and milk on the floor. Someone dropped their tray. I sink back down into my seat just in time to catch Emily shrugging her shoulders at Casley like I'm some kind of weirdo she can't figure out.

Another piece of my heart splinters away.

"Hey, I know what would *totally* cheer up this day," Emily says, a conspiratorial smile on her face.

If you vanished? I think to myself, then immediately feel bad. Girls should be nice to other girls. Lift them up instead of tearing them down, as Mom would say. Besides, Emily hasn't done anything wrong, really.

I pull my face into a reluctant smile. I can do this. I might be tired and stressed out, but I can give Emily another chance to show me why Casley likes her so much. "Okay. What?"

"Makeup Monday!" Emily chirps in response. She reaches into her bag and unloads a handful of different tubes and bottles onto the table. They clatter down, drawing attention from everyone around us. Moisturizers, foundations, powders, even an eyelash curler. It looks terrifying.

With a final flourish, Emily pulls a small lipstick out of her bag and holds it up for us to inspect. "Today, we have"—she turns the tube upside down to read the small label on the bottom—"Déjà Vu!"

Casley squeals and snatches the lipstick out of Emily's hand. She removes the lid and slowly rolls the stick of color up until we can all see it. "Ohhhh, it's perfect!"

I stare at the lipstick, stupefied. It's a vivid color that reminds me of cranberries at Christmastime. I guess it's pretty, but it's lipstick.

Casley runs the tube over her already glossy lips, then smacks them together. Along with her perfect skin and honey-colored hair, the lipstick makes her look sophisticated. Glamorous. Neither of which I am. She passes the lipstick to Emily, who does the same, and then the tube ends up in front of me. I stare at it, torn between putting it on just to fit in and hurling it toward the nearest trash can. Blinking my weary eyes at the pile of makeup on the table, I sigh.

"If you're worried about animal cruelty, don't be," Emily says, sensing my hesitation. "Mom always got the scoop on samples before she brought them home, and these were *not* tested on bunnies or mice or anything."

I push the tube away from me, irritated. This is who Casley wants to hang out with instead of me? My heart is pounding even though the rest of my body feels slow and sluggish. I can't believe this! I have to go home today and face a bunch of wet clothes, sleep in a closet, *and* try to keep Dad from noticing. And Casley? She'll be doing this—playing dress-up and giggling with Emily. It's not fair.

"I'm *not* worried about bunnies," I snap suddenly.

The table goes uncomfortably silent. Emily's cranberry lips part in a dismayed O shape.

"Sorry. I just mean that I don't think this color will go well with my...um...my..." I stop talking, realizing it's useless. This is *exactly* why I didn't want to sit here.

Suddenly, I feel hot, like someone has struck a match somewhere inside me. My entire body flushes with annoyance.

"Never mind," I spit out. "I gotta go."

I could walk away quietly. In fact, I know I should, but I'm so hurt that I don't. Right now, Emily seems like the best person to blame for the bad stuff that's been happening to me. If she hadn't stolen Casley away, I would've been at her house Saturday night. Dad wouldn't have made me go on his dumb tour bus. A ghost wouldn't have followed me home! Oh yeah, and I also would've gotten more than a few hours of sleep last night.

It's all too much.

"You know what?" I raise my voice over the hum of conversation around us. "I just had the worst weekend of my life, and you're here acting like a stupid tube of lipstick is going to fix it. Well, it won't. Thanks so much for *not* understanding, as usual."

Snatching my tray from the table, I dump my lunch into the trash and then slam it into the tray return. The sound echoes through the cafeteria like a firework. Conversations stop, forks hover in midair, and everyone—I mean *everyone*—looks at me. Including Warner.

Casley's eyes meet mine. They're filled with shock. I wait for her to get up, to follow me so we can talk this through like we always used to, but she slowly shakes her head and looks back down at her tray instead.

She's made her choice, and it's not me.

TWELVE

I keep to myself the rest of the day. It's hard walking down the halls alone, knowing everyone I pass is whispering about me, the weird girl who freaked out at lunch.

What a nightmare.

Sniffling back tears, I finally trudge up the stairs of my building at the end of the day. My phone chimes for about the eleven-hundredth time, and although I've been ignoring it all afternoon, I finally look at the screen.

Casley: R U OK?

Casley: what is going on?

Casley: can we talk?

Casley: what did you mean by worst weekend of your life?

Casley: just text me back. Please?

The list of messages goes on and on. I should be thankful

that at least Casley still cares enough to check on me, but I can't shake my disappointment. If she cares so much, why didn't she leave the cafeteria with me? Probably because I was a giant jerk. My stomach churns as I replay what I said to Emily in my head. It wasn't fair, and I know it.

Slamming my backpack down in the living room, I fall face-first onto the couch. I haven't felt this terrible in a long time, and that's saying something, since I walked from first period to second period with toilet paper hanging out of my shorts earlier this year.

"Mom? Dad?" I call out.

Nothing. The wind picks up outside, and something pings off our large front window. A branch, maybe? I flip over onto my back and glance at the window. The sky is dark. It was nice out on my way home, sunny and cheerful. Now it's what Casley would call a hot mess out there. Awesome. I'm already nervous about being home alone after what happened on Saturday night, and a brewing storm doesn't exactly ease my nerves. It's like the perfect recipe for a horror movie.

I hate horror movies.

I slip off my sneakers one at a time. They thunk against the floor, and although I really should get up and put them away, I can't. I'm paralyzed. Too many thoughts racing around in my head. Too many feelings. Warner Jameson saw my temper tantrum in the cafeteria today. Warner. Freakin'. Jameson. I tell myself I'm not allowed to cry about this anymore because it's my fault to begin with, but it's hard. How am I going to face everyone tomorrow?

I shut my eyes and enjoy the darkness for a moment. I'm so tired that even with my brain working overtime, I could probably fall asleep anywhere right now. I've just drifted off when a draft suddenly rips through the room, startling me awake again. I grab the back cushion of the couch and pull myself upright, confused.

Icy fingers of air creep across my cheeks and neck. I stand up. A bigger gust of ice-cold air flips my ponytail around, then rushes up the back of my oversized sweatshirt. I clap a hand over my mouth to keep from screaming. This isn't from the back door being open. I can *feel* it.

A quiet scratching sound begins in the wall. Like before, it quickly grows louder and more frantic.

Scritch scratch.

Scritch scratch.

Scritch scratch. Scritch scratch. Scritch scratch. Scritch scratch. Scritch scratch.

I cover my ears, hoping to block it out. It doesn't work. Instead, the scratching builds until it seems to be coming from every corner of the room. I'm trapped.

I look up just in time to see one of Mom's framed pictures suddenly tumble from the wall to the floor. Then a stack of papers Dad left on the coffee table whips up into the air like they're taking flight. I clench my eyes shut, remembering the way my yellow curtains bounced around two nights ago like floppy, pale puppets on strings.

Please stop. Please, please, please. I think the words over and over, hoping it'll make a difference.

The draft dies down, and I force my eyes back open. The room is a disaster zone. Several pictures are down, coasters and papers are scattered everywhere, and even the fresh flowers from the vase are lying on the floor. I press myself against the wall and take a minute to breathe.

Making my way around the room on rubbery legs, I pick everything up. Most of the stuff is okay, except for one picture. I turn it over gently in my hands and groan at the splintered frame. It's our most recent family photograph. Mom had us all dress up and go to the pond to have it taken. It was such a pain and *really* boring, but the picture is nice. I push the jagged edges of the wood back together tightly and make a mental note to use some glue on it later. Mom still might notice, but it isn't unfixable.

Just when I think my heart is returning to a normal, steady beat, I notice the small desk where Mom keeps her computer. It looks perfect. Untouched. Dozens of recipe cards are still neatly stacked on top, sticky notes dangle from Mom's open laptop screen, and a pyramid of Jenga pieces are perfectly balanced on top of one another. A stack of Dad's research papers is sitting right in the center of the dark wood, staring up at me.

Weird. How did all that stuff stay on the desk when the breeze was strong enough to knock framed pictures off the walls? Scientifically, it doesn't seem possible. Sticky notes aren't even all that sticky. Oh, and anyone who has played Jenga for like five minutes knows how lopsided and stupid those little wooden pieces are! They should have blown off the desk. It *all* should have blown off the desk.

I'm officially terrified. The word *ghost* surfaces in my brain again, sending a bolt of panic through my body. Could a ghost really be responsible for this? And what about the wet clothes in my dresser? Did he do that, too?

Digging through my backpack, I pull out my phone again. The low-battery symbol flashes once, twice, three times, and then the screen goes dark. No! No, no, no! I punch at the screen with my index finger, fear gripping me in a choke hold. I was so tired last night that I forgot to plug it in before I crawled into the closet. So much for calling Mom and Dad, unless I go upstairs and get my charger. I glance at the stairwell. It's dark. Maybe my phone can wait.

The first drops of rain begin to fall outside. Fat, loud drops. Thunder rattles the windows. Lightning flashes, sending jolts of light racing across the living room walls. I tug the hood of my sweatshirt over my head. I know I should act mature about this. But I don't feel mature right now. *I feel scared.*

A soft groan starts up somewhere deep in the floor. It's low and disturbing. It's one of those sounds that my mom would say is just "the house settling," but I know what Dad would say. Houses don't settle. Ghosts do. They settle into graveyards, alleys, tombs, and maybe even rooms with pale yellow curtains. Fear fills my veins with ice as everything around me grows darker. I can't tell if it's the paint on the walls that's changing or if the bulbs above my head are growing dimmer, but one thing is for sure: I'm not alone in this room.

Grabbing my dead cell phone, I race up the stairs. The bathroom—I have to get to the bathroom. It's the only room in the entire house with a lock on the door. The hallway light is flickering on and off, making it hard to get up the steps without falling. The groaning sound is louder now, making the walls hum with an energy I'm afraid of. A bad energy.

I run into the bathroom and slam the door behind me. Locking it, I slide down the wood until my butt hits the floor. I'm terrified, and I have no idea what to do.

"Please come home, someone," I whisper to myself. I

can't hear the groaning sound from in here, but that doesn't matter. It doesn't matter, because I realize that for the first time in about six years, the shower curtain is pulled shut. It's *never* shut. Sam had a dream when he was little that he came into the bathroom one morning and the shower curtain was closed. When he opened it, he found a skeleton in there. Silly as it sounds, the dream scared him so bad that he's pulled it open every single day since then. I know, because I've teased him about it every single day.

I could leave this room and make a break for my bedroom, but what's the point? If I truly am being haunted, a different room isn't going to change anything. Whatever this ghost wants, it obviously thinks I have the answer.

I'm the one the boy on the bus was staring at.

I'm the one he kept trying to talk to.

I'm the one who always said that ghosts aren't real.

I'm the one who acted like Dad was ridiculous when he told stories that made my skin crawl and my heart race.

I did something a scientist should never, *ever* do. I ignored my instincts, the instincts that told me I was right to be afraid. I was so caught up in trying to cover up my fear that I pretended it wasn't there. How could I have been so wrong?

Sliding across the floor on my butt, I reach a hand toward the shower curtain. I have to pull it back. If there's any bravery left in me at all, I need to find it. My hand is shaking so badly I can barely grip the plastic. When I finally find my courage, I give a hard yank. The curtain slides across, the sound of metal loops on a metal rod echoing off the walls. I see white tiles. I see shampoo. I see soap.

I see writing.

Time stops as I stare at the jagged black number scribbled on the wall. It's lopsided and crooked and a million times more frightening than the flickering lights and fluttering curtains. It's the number that haunts me at night. The number the little boy on the bus left for me to find. The number that confirms my worst fear. The number 396.

THIRTEEN

I'm still slumped against the bathroom door when someone knocks on it. My muscles tense.

"Claire?" My father's voice carries through the thick wood. "You in there?"

"Dad!" I breathe out, scrambling up off the floor. I fling open the door and toss myself into his arms.

"Whoa, whoa, whoa. What's going on?"

I open my mouth to answer him, then remember I can't. If Dad finds out I think a spirit followed me home from the tour, there's no telling what he might do. I could wake up one day to find that our house has become one of his tour stops or that he's writing a new book with a character named Claire. It's not that I don't trust him. Not exactly, anyway. It's just that I know how excited he gets about this stuff. A ghostly happening in our house would be impossible for him to ignore, even if that meant making things worse for me.

Glancing back into the bathroom, I breathe a sigh of relief that I had the good sense to close the shower curtain again so he doesn't see the number. Like the soaking-wet clothes in my dresser, I'd never be able to explain that away.

He puts his hands on my shoulders and gently rotates me so I'm looking at him. "Claire, you're scaring me. Is everything okay?"

I shake off the fear that's settled into my bones. "Yeah. I just got a little creeped out with the storm is all."

Dad's eyebrows furrow. "Storm? What storm?"

"The thunder and lightning. I guess I just didn't want to be home alone during that."

Dad scratches his head and walks to the end of the hall. There's a small window there. Pulling the curtain aside, he looks at me. The sun is out and brighter than ever. No wind. No rain. No thunder. Only sun.

"What? How?" I walk over to the window and look out for myself. The pavement in the alley is dry; there's not even a hint of those big ugly raindrops I saw earlier. My legs go wobbly.

This can't be happening.

"Honey, are you okay? You're worrying me." Dad is

staring at me like I've got three eyeballs now. I might as well have. I definitely don't have a working brain.

Taking one last look at the beautiful weather outside, I nod. I'm really not okay, but he needs to believe I am. The last thing I want is for him to figure out our house is probably— scratch that, *definitely*—haunted. No. I need to deal with this myself.

I smile at him. "I'm fine. Just a little confused. That's what I get for coming home from school and falling asleep for a few minutes. I'm all groggy now."

Dad laughs. "I've been there. It's like waking up and being in the Twilight Zone."

Right. The Twilight Zone. I have no clue what that is, but I nod anyway.

"I better get started on my homework. Love ya." I give him a chipper wave, then head to my room. Shutting the door behind me, I wait until I hear his footsteps get quieter. Once I can't hear them anymore, I open my door again. No way am I going to be alone with this ghost.

~~~

I've just settled into my bed with a book when a shadow moves in front of my door. This time, it's a fourteen-year-old boy shadow. Sam. I stare at him. He stares at me. Then he comes in and closes the door. I almost complain, but the grave look on his face tells me not to.

"You gonna tell me what happened in the cafeteria today?" he asks softly. Reaching up, he flips his ratty old Cubs cap backward. I can see his face better now. It's worried.

"How do you know about that?"

"Seriously? Everyone knows about it, Claire. Jake's teacher let him go down to the cafeteria to grab lunch early since he had to leave for a doctor's appointment. According to him, you flipped out and started yelling."

"Jake is a gossip," I snap.

"Jake is *honest*," he retorts. "He wasn't trying to be a jerk. He actually seemed kinda worried."

Guilt bubbles up in me all over again. No matter what I do, I'll never forget how I acted in the cafeteria or the hurt look on Emily's face. I was mean.

"Don't worry about it," I answer. The things I want to say to my brother are buried somewhere, but I can't quite shake them free. Maybe it's embarrassment. Maybe it's because admitting Casley is moving on without me makes it feel more real. I don't know. But something keeps me from telling him the truth, even though I know I should. "Nothing happened."

"That's a lie, and we both know it." Sam settles onto my

bed with a sigh. "I'm your brother, Claire. I know you better than anyone else, even if you don't want me to."

He's right. Of all the people in the world, Sam knows me best. He knows when I'm mad. When I'm jealous. When I'm sad. Sometimes he knows things before I do. I guess that's bound to happen when you're so close together in age. It's never bothered me before, but today it does. My secrets don't feel like secrets anymore.

"I just have a lot going on," I blurt out.

"All right," he responds. "Maybe you'd feel better about whatever it is if you *talked* to Casley about it. Have you tried that?"

I sigh. "I can't, Sam. She's too busy with her new friend— trying on makeup and completely changing her wardrobe."

"Makeup? Doesn't sound like Cas to me."

"Yeah, well, it is. She's changed, Sam. She's changed, and I'm on the outside now." The familiar sting of tears makes me reach for a tissue. I hate this. I hate that everything is changing and I don't have any control over it.

A long moment of silence stretches out. Sam just stares at me, his lips pressed into a frustrated line. Finally, he takes a deep breath, kicks his shoes off, and settles further onto my bed. "Okay. So try me, then."

My eyes snap to his. "What?"

"Try *me*," he repeats. "If you can't talk to Casley about whatever is bothering you, then talk to me."

"You won't be able to help."

"How do you know?" His voice sounds strained now. Like he's trying not to get angry with me, but it's hard. I don't blame him. I feel like a jerk. "You haven't tried."

I look him straight in the eyes. "I know because I don't think you'll believe me. That's why."

The room is silent. Birds chirp outside. I'd enjoy hearing them if it weren't for the feeling that they are somehow the calm before the storm. Something bad is coming, and I have no idea how to stop it.

"It has to do with the ghost tour, doesn't it?" he asks. His eyes darken as he watches me for a reaction. "You've been weird since you came back from that. Quiet. Moody."

"I've been a jerk. I know," I grumble. I take a deep breath and tell myself it's time to spill the beans. Sam is stubborn; he'll just keep bugging me until I cave anyway.

I get up and double-check that my door is fully closed. If I am going to talk to Sam about this, no one can hear us. Especially Dad.

"Yes. It's about the tour. Since I came home from it, *things* have been happening."

"What kinds of things?" Sam asks, one eyebrow raised.

"A little boy showed up on the ghost tour bus. No one else saw him. Then he vanished. He left a piece of paper on the ground by his seat with the number three hundred and ninety-six on it."

Sam looks at the ceiling like he's thinking about what I've just told him. He's probably considering whether or not to run. "And you think he's...what? *Haunting* you?"

He says "haunting" like it's a four-letter word. It might as well be. It sounds ridiculous. I know that.

"I know how it sounds, but there's this feeling. A horrible feeling. I can't explain it, but I know the boy caused it. He also did some bad things here in the house."

I tug him into a standing position and pull him toward the bathroom. I've got to show him the number on the shower wall. He'll understand then. He has to.

"Wait, what are we doing in here?" Sam asks, eyeing the closed shower curtain warily. As if out of habit, he reaches to pull it open.

"Sam! Wait until I explain!" I try to grab his wrist, but I'm too late. He flings open the curtain before I can stop him.

A hiss of shock escapes him as the jagged black numbers appear.

"What is this? What does this even mean? Is this written in *Sharpie*?"

Sam backs up, brings a hand to his chest, and leans against the wall.

I run my hand over the tiles, wincing at the stark black marring them. "I think so."

"But you didn't do this?" he asks.

I drop my hands to my hips and give him a questioning look. "Why would I scribble a number in Sharpie on our bathroom wall, Sam?"

"I don't know!" He flings his hands in the air and paces around. "I'm just trying to figure out what's going on around here!"

Sam runs both hands down his face and sighs. "I was going to eat the rest of the cookies and play Fortnite when I got home. How did I get from that to"—he jabs a finger toward the writing on the wall—"this?"

I laugh darkly. "You're not the only one whose night has been ruined. I barely survived a tornado in our living room!"

My brother cocks a head to the side, confused, but I don't have the energy to explain it to him. "Look, I didn't bring you in here and show you this just so you'd lose your precious gaming time. I showed you because three hundred and ninety-six is the same number that was on the paper I found on the bus."

Just thinking about the faded paper the boy on the bus left behind makes my palms go clammy and my knees get that limp-noodle feeling. My mom always says that onions, carrots, and celery are the "trifecta of cooking." Right now, I'm sad, tired, and confused—the trifecta of feelings, if there is such a thing.

"It's a ghost, Sam," I whisper, tears spilling onto my cheeks without warning. "I know it sounds unbelievable, but... it's a ghost."

"Hey, it's okay. I believe you," my brother says softly. "I'll help. I promise."

I look at him through the haze of tears and smile. "You will?"

"Yup. But after this, you gotta swear that you'll try to fix things with Casley. She's your best friend, Claire. You can't let some makeup come between you."

Sam is right. I know he is. But it isn't that simple. After how I acted today, I wouldn't be surprised if Casley never wanted to speak to me again.

FOURTEEN

My bedroom door is shut, and I've jammed a chair under the knob. Can't be too safe when you're talking about ghosts. Especially in this house. Sam and I are sitting on the floor, a half dozen of Dad's books spread out in front of us like a map to the unknown.

"I've tried to think of another explanation for what is happening, but I can't," I say. "I don't think there is one."

Sam considers this for a moment. "Let's just start at the beginning. If it *is* a ghost, do you have any idea who it could be?"

"Not really. The tour bus only stopped at three places, so the ghost has to have come from one of them, right?"

"I guess." He opens the notebook in front of him to a blank piece of paper. "What were the places?"

"The Alley of Death, Hull-House, and the Couch Tomb."
I count them off on my fingers.

Sam stiffens a little. "Gahhhh. *The Alley of Death?* That's dark, even for Dad."

I flip the book closed. "If you think it sounds bad, you should see it. It's awful." Watching the lines deepen in his forehead, I frown. "You know you don't have to do this, right?"

"I know. I'm good. Besides, if I wake up some night and there's a ghost in my room, I'll definitely regret not helping you."

True story.

He sticks the eraser end of a pencil in his mouth, then draws it back out and taps it against his leg. Gross.

"You saw more than three places, though, right? Did you just drive by the other spots or something?"

"Yup," I clarify. "Dad slowed down, and a few times he pulled over to the side of the street while he talked about a location."

"But you don't think a ghost from one of those drive-by places could be the one haunting you now?" Sam asks.

"I don't know. But if it is, then I'm in *big* trouble. We drove past a lot of places that night. Figuring out who the ghost is from that mess would take forever."

Sam shakes his head. "Not really. The ghost can only be a

little boy, right? So we research the locations you visited where a little boy died, and we should have our answer!"

I think on this. He's right. Mostly, anyway. The ghost was definitely a boy. But Chicago is an old city, and according to Dad, a lot of scary stuff has happened here. Fires. Diseases. Gangsters. I bet a little boy died at some point in history at every single one of those locations. Not good. Not good at all.

"Something did happen when we stopped at Hull-House," I offer.

"What?"

"I thought I heard something. Then I saw a shadow through the window, like someone moving around on the bus after everyone else had gotten off. I searched it, but there was no one there."

Sam sits up straighter. "Well, that has to be it, then! That has to be the spot the ghost came from!"

I wave my hands around in front of my brother. "Slow down. I don't think it's that simple. I didn't actually *see* the ghost boy clearly until the very end of the tour when we were done with all the stops. We were leaving the Couch Tomb by then. He could have gotten on the bus while we were looking at it, but since I saw the shadow before that, isn't it possible he got on at one of the earlier stops and stayed hidden?"

Sam is quiet for a minute. Too long in Sam time.

"Hey." I knock on the side of his head. "You still with me?"

Swiping my hand away, he nods. "Yeah. I was just wondering why you haven't told Dad about this. He can be annoying about this stuff, but he knows more than we do about it. I bet he could figure out what's going on."

"I don't want him to know," I say firmly. "He'll use what's happening to me for a new book or tour or something."

Sam tosses a book into the pile, then flashes me an exasperated look. "He wouldn't do that."

"You didn't see his tour, Sam! The people are *obsessed* with ghosts. They're willing to pay almost seventy dollars for two hours on a bus in Chicago traffic! Dad is always complaining about bills. Mom, too. If it meant that the Spirits bus would make more money, I think he'd totally add our house as a stop."

I cringe, imagining a whole tour group filled with people like Lens Cap Guy and Toga Woman taking pictures outside my bedroom window while I'm trying to do homework or watch TV. Sam might think Dad would never do that to us, but he's wrong. Telling him about this would be like dangling a steak in front of a hungry dog.

"*Okay*. You sure that's the only reason you don't want to tell Dad?" Sam presses, one eyebrow raised doubtfully.

Unease pricks at me. "What are you talking about? What other reason would there be?"

He shrugs. "I dunno. I thought maybe you might be sorta...afraid of Dad's ghost stories? When he starts talking about them, you usually leave."

When I don't say anything right away, Sam continues. "Don't be mad, but I know that the alley isn't the only place you count. I've heard you through the wall between our rooms, counting to yourself. It's almost always after Dad has been telling us about his research."

Suddenly, I'm not uneasy anymore. I'm angry. "Wait. You heard me counting in the alley? I knew it. I *knew* you were spying on me!"

Sam immediately lifts both hands in the air, palms facing me as if he's surrendering. "No. It wasn't like that. I already told you I wasn't spying on you."

"Then explain how you know that!" I demand. "Explain how you know about something I do when I think I'm alone!"

What a nightmare. I teased Sam relentlessly when I found out about the shower curtain thing. No way is he going to let this go without making fun of me for at least a week.

"You know how we used to go on a family bike ride every Sunday?" Sam asks.

I nod, curling in on myself. We store the bikes in the basement. The dark, dank, *horrible* basement. It's another place I count to keep myself from getting scared. Somehow,

Sam must have heard me. Now I know he's heard me through the wall between our rooms, too. Embarrassment creeps up into my cheeks.

His eyes soften. "Dude, it's not a big deal to be scared of something. I'm scared of plenty of stuff."

"I'm not scared." Scientists don't get scared. They don't have to count to get a bike out of the basement or to walk through the alley. They don't feel light-headed and afraid on ghost tours. They don't have to ask their parents to solve their problems. Scientists gather data, analyze it, then fix their own problems.

Except this problem is the biggest one I've ever had. It's bigger than the time I spilled grape juice on our new carpet, then panicked and used an armchair to cover it. It's bigger than my problems with Casley. It's so big I don't know where to start, or if I even can.

"Telling Dad doesn't make you, like, weak or whatever. He might be able to help," Sam says.

I hold a hand up. "Stop. You might be..." I swallow hard, barely able to form the words. "You might be a little bit right, but that doesn't change anything. I still don't want to tell Dad."

Because if we do, it will be like throwing gasoline on a fire. Things are bad now, but if Dad hears about this new ghost, he'll *never* stop with the scary stuff. I swallow hard, unable to think of anything worse than being surrounded by Dad's ghosts twenty-four seven—not even the rumors at school.

No. We can't tell Dad, because if we do, eventually there won't be anywhere I can go without counting.

FIFTEEN

The first time I counted because I was afraid was when I was six or seven. We had just moved into our house, and every day a different set of people showed up to fix it. Painters. Electricians. Carpenters. I remember coming out of my room one morning, stumbling over cardboard boxes and only half-awake, when the lights in the hallway started flickering. The bare walls flashed in front of my bleary eyes, highlighting the peeling wallpaper and abandoned nails hanging from it like rotting teeth.

I remember Mom finding me frozen there, shaking me gently, and telling me that the flickering was just the electrician working out some "kinks" in the wiring. I also remember counting. I was on 412 when she found me.

I guess I've been counting ever since. I'd rather explain what's happening around me with a microscope or a test tube or a strip of litmus paper, but when that isn't possible, I get nervous. The feeling is overwhelming, like being in the deep end of a pool and realizing you can't swim. That's when the counting helps. It slows down my racing brain. It evens out my breathing. It makes me braver. It also really, *really* embarrasses me.

Guess I didn't realize anyone else knew about it. Part of me wishes Sam hadn't noticed my counting, but part of me is relieved. Maybe it isn't as weird as I think it is. Maybe it's okay for scientists to be afraid sometimes, too. Maybe my brother is actually a decent human in disguise.

Nah.

Sam claps his hands, startling me from my thoughts. "Okay, forget Dad. I still don't agree with you, but I get it. I won't tell him if you don't want me to."

"Thank you," I whisper.

"Let's go over this one more time in case we missed something. Was there anything interesting about the little boy you saw? Anything we can use to figure out his identity?"

"Like forming a hypothesis," I say, taking some small comfort in the fact that unraveling this mystery might not be that different from doing a science experiment. Why didn't I think of it before? "Sam! We can use the scientific method to figure this out!"

My brother scoffs. "Please tell me you're joking, Claire."

"No, hear me out. This could totally work! There are five main steps in the scientific method." I count off the steps on my fingers so he can see them. "Observation, research, hypothesis, experiment, and conclusion! We already observed our problem—the ghost."

Sam shoots me a *duh* look.

"And we already started the research. C'mon," I plead. "This is our best chance at solving the mystery, and you know it. I might not know much about ghosts, but I know a lot about science."

Sam smirks. "All right. Calm down, brainiac. For once, I actually agree with you."

Punching him playfully, I allow myself to smile. Maybe this ghost isn't going to be the end of me after all.

"What about the experiment part, though?" Concern flickers across his face. "How're you going to do that? Unless we lure the ghost here so we can see him."

Lure the ghost here? My muscles go rigid at the idea. "He's already been here, Sam. The whole point of this is to keep him from coming back."

"I know that, but I wasn't on the bus when the boy showed up, so I couldn't help with the observation step, you know? That's all you. And since you don't want to summon him, we can't get more evidence."

"Summon?" I can't help it; I snicker. "You know who you sound like?"

"If you say Dad, I'm walking out of here."

I cut my laugh short, then pull a grave look onto my face. "Of course not!"

He stands to leave, but I tug him back down to the floor. "Kidding!"

"Whatever. Joke all you want, but I'd get your nerdy little scientist hat on fast, because out of the two of us, the ghost chose you, Claire. Not me."

His words sober me. The ghost *did* choose me, and if I don't figure out what he wants, he's never going to go away. He's already wrecked the living room, damaged our family picture, and written on our bathroom wall in permanent marker! Oh, and let's not forget my soggy wardrobe. If the ghost has already done that much bad stuff around here, who knows what he'll do next.

I sit up straighter and will myself to remember that night. The stupid logos we stuck to the bus. The Alley of Death. The mausoleum.

The boy on the bus.

A lost memory slowly comes into focus and clicks into place. The clothes. "He was wearing a suit! It was old-fashioned. Definitely not something a kid would wear now. Maybe if I can figure out how old it is—"

"—then we can figure out how long ago the ghost was alive!" Sam finishes for me. We high-five, and I grin at him. When we're not trying to kill each other, we're a pretty good team.

"Hey, I'm sorry about what happened in the alley, by the way," he says suddenly.

I'd almost forgotten about that. It seems like so long ago. "It's okay. I scared myself more than you did, anyway."

"Yeah, well, I shouldn't have been out there." He exhales loudly, like there's something on his mind. "I was thinking about throwing a test in the dumpster so Mom and Dad wouldn't see it."

Whoa. Hiding a test from Mom and Dad is a pretty big deal. Sam didn't seem nervous when I saw him. He was just tossing that crumpled-up paper ball back and forth like he didn't have a care in the world. Tricky boy.

"Did you?"

Sam looks at me quizzically. "Did I what?"

"Throw the test away."

He shakes his head. "Nope. I showed it to them that night. I failed my pre-algebra test."

Failed? I'm speechless. Sam is one of the smartest guys I know. Math isn't his favorite subject, but I've never known him to do badly in it. In anything, really.

"What happened?"

He tosses his hands up in the air, then lets them fall back into his lap. "I'm not sure. It's hard, you know? Math is so black and white. There's just a right answer and a wrong answer." He looks down, sadness washing over his face. "Somehow, my answers always seem to be wrong."

Suddenly, I feel bad for him. Worse than I feel for myself. "I'm not great at math, but I'm okay. Like, I got a B on the last test, and I'm in the advanced seventh-grade class. Maybe I could help?"

He doesn't answer.

"C'mon, I owe you at least that. You know, for helping me figure out who the ghost boy is."

It takes him a minute, but Sam finally nods. "Cool. Thanks."

Wow. We're agreeing again. Weird.

"Okay, so back to the ghost."

Sam grins. I catch it out of the corner of my eye, and I smile, too. Even if we never get along again, this has been a nice moment.

"Where were your three stops again?"

"The Alley of Death," I say, stopping when he puts his hand in the air.

"Any children die there?"

I drag out *Spirits of Chicago* and thumb to the page about

the Iroquois Theater fire. "The play that was showing that day was *Mr. Bluebeard*. I guess it was a children's play. So, yeah. This says a lot of kids died. Like, more than two hundred."

My brother winces. "That's terrible. But helpful. Since that was one of the stops on the bus tour, isn't it possible that the ghost was one of those two hundred?"

I think about the white suit the ghost wore. Snatching up my laptop, I begin Googling "old-timey suits." A bunch of pictures of men in suits come up. Sam laughs.

"Try 'vintage boys' suits,'" he suggests.

I type the words in and gasp at what pops up. Dozens of suits, some of them black, but many of them brown. I click on one that looks like what I *think* the boy was wearing. Knickerbockers. Weird name, even weirder pants. They're puffy and come midway up the boy in the picture's calves. Like capris, only fluffier. My hands shake. This is it. This looks like what the boy was wearing. I only got one real look at the boy's legs, but it doesn't take much to remember clothes like these. They're too unusual to forget.

"It says here that these pants were popular in the early 1900s," Sam reads, following the sentence on my screen with his finger.

"Early 1900s. Ugh." I rub my tired eyes. This is going to be even harder than I thought.

"What?"

"According to Dad's tour, that's when *everything* bad happened in Chicago! The Iroquois Theater fire happened in 1903. Hull-House became 'haunted' with the devil baby in 1913. The woman they *think* was Resurrection Mary died in 1934." I stop there, but the list goes on and on. Even though a ghost is after me, I'm beginning to feel very grateful I didn't live in Chicago in the early 1900s. Clearly, that was a freaky time.

"So, you're saying that doesn't narrow things down at all, then?" He sounds disappointed.

"Sorta. I just think we'll need to do a lot more research to solve this. That's all." I look over at his pale face. "You sure you're up for this?"

"You sure you're going to help me with my pre-algebra?"

"Yup."

He gives me a fist bump. "Then let's do this."

SIXTEEN

Two hours later, my eyes are tired, my fingers are brittle from turning pages, and my brain is completely fried. Like, need-a-transplant-if-I'm-ever-going-to-think-again fried. I stop pacing and fall backward onto my bed.

"You gonna be okay?" Sam asks. He's got a pile of Snickers wrappers around him now. "Because you look freaking awful."

"Thanks," I fire back sarcastically. "Hey, I forgot to tell you about the other stuff that happened before you came home. Not sure if those things can be considered clues or not, though."

He cocks his head to the side. "What stuff?"

"Well, besides the number written in the bathroom, the ghost also flooded my dresser. Like, literally filled it with water so all of my clothes are wet."

I sigh, thinking about how I haven't done anything about

my clothes yet. I meant to put them in the washer when I got home, but that was before the writing on the shower wall showed up. Now I'll be stuck wearing dirty things to school tomorrow. With my luck, Warner will notice. How could he not?

"Oh, he also knocked our family picture off the wall and broke it," I add, suddenly remembering the wind that tore through our living room.

"Mom know?"

"Not yet, but she will. The frame totally broke. I'll be able to glue it, but you'll be able to see where the wood splintered."

"Huh. Even if those things are clues, they're both really sucky. Wet clothes? Weird. And there are dozens of pictures in the house; why did the ghost break just one? Then there's the three hundred and ninety-six... I don't get it."

"Me neither," I admit, feeling more overwhelmed by the minute. "Ugh, Sam. Mom and Dad are going to find out. I just know it."

"Relax. They aren't going to find out. We can handle the screwed-up stuff. You take care of the wet clothes and gluing the frame. I'll deal with the shower wall, okay?"

I lift an eyebrow in doubt. "You know how to get Sharpie off tile?"

"Not yet, but I'll figure it out. It can't be that—"

A voice echoes up the stairs, interrupting him. It's Mom.

Dinnertime. I've been ignoring my growling stomach for a while now. Not easy when your foodie mother is downstairs cooking something that smells like Thanksgiving.

"Good timing," I say. "We need to take a break."

Sam rubs his eyes. There are dark circles underneath. "Agreed. But I think we made some progress."

We did, just not enough to answer any real questions. If the little boy from the bus was one of the children who died in the Iroquois Theater fire, it will take us weeks to figure out who he was. Maybe months. And that's assuming it's even possible. I don't have that kind of time. Not with Ghost Boy finding new ways to tear up my life every day.

"I know you don't want to hear this," he says, cracking my door open. "But I don't think we should be ruling out girls yet."

"Girls didn't wear suits like that, Sam."

That, and the ghost didn't look like a girl. A shiver races through me as I remember the boy's sad face and dark eyes.

"So you're convinced the ghost is a boy?" Sam asks.

"I am. One hundred percent."

"Then tonight I'll do some research in bed. I'll send you anything I find."

I wrestle my brother into a bear hug. He tries to worm his way out, but I hold on tight. "Thank you. And keep your door locked!"

He tugs free of my grip and straightens the baseball cap I knocked crooked. "No prob. And I will, but do you really think that's going to stop a gh—"

"Stop what?" My mom appears in the doorway.

Sam startles, then quickly kicks the book closest to him beneath my bed. "Mom! Jeez, you scared me."

She laughs and moves into the room, then ruffles his hair. I notice that Sam is at least an inch taller than she is now. How did that happen? More importantly, why am I still so short?

"I'm sorry I scared you, sweetie. Didn't know if you two heard me calling you for dinner." She wipes at a spot on her cheek, and I laugh. It's flour.

"Homemade rolls?" I ask hopefully.

She nods. "Fresh out of the oven just now. Get down there soon, or your father is going to inhale them all!"

Sam and I exchange a look and race for the door at the same time. He gets there first, throwing an arm out and shoving me back. I skid across my hardwood floor like a hockey puck. Squealing, I chase after him. It's no use, though; he's got a head start, and the stairwell is narrow. I'm done for. And so are those rolls!

We hit the kitchen in a running, squalling mess. Sam first, me second, and Mom the calm, smiling caboose. She looks so proud. I think us loving her cooking makes her even happier than seeing orders roll in for her online bakery.

Dad holds his hands up as if he's shielding himself. "Hey! Slow down, you two!"

We screech to a halt. Sam snags a roll and stuffs it in his mouth before plopping down. I scrunch my face up at him, hoping he gets the drift that shoving a roll the size of a baseball into his mouth all at once is disgusting.

When everyone has taken their seat, food is passed around. No wonder it smelled like Thanksgiving in here. It pretty much is! Mashed potatoes and gravy, green bean casserole, sweet potatoes, and Greek roasted chicken. Mom really went all out tonight. I'm just about to cram a fluffy bite of potato in my mouth when she clinks her fork against a water glass.

"I want us all to take a minute to congratulate your father on a third printing of his book," she says, raising her glass in the air. "We're so proud of you, David."

Dad lifts his glass. Sam and I do, too. Then we all clink them in the middle, trying to ignore the water that sloshes out onto our good tablecloth.

"Thank you, guys. What a nice surprise!" Dad beams at my mother. Maybe their midnight money talks are over. Maybe he'll give up the Spirits bus and stop writing these awful books. "I wasn't going to tell everyone just yet because

I just started my research, but my publisher is so happy with how the first book is doing that they've asked me to write a second one!"

Oh. No.

Mom squeals and throws her arms around him. Sam eyes me warily. I shrug and try to keep my face blank so Dad can't see my horror. So much for thinking his ghost obsession might die down soon. If he writes a second book, this whole nightmare will get much, much worse. He'll find new ghosts to tell us about. Ghosts worse than the one that's already haunting me.

"I can't believe it!" Mom claps her hands together, beaming. "All of this started with your research on Inez Clarke—remember that?"

I remember that. The story of Inez Clarke is one of the more frightening ones Dad has told me. Rumor has it that she was killed by lightning when she was seven, and every time it storms, the statue marking her grave *vanishes*. Dad said dozens of groundskeepers have quit working at Graceland Cemetery, where she's buried, because of the stories...and the sounds, like a little girl crying.

Taking a deep breath, I focus on my mashed potatoes. My heart is racing. My palms are clammy. If I wasn't sitting in a brightly lit room surrounded by my family right now, I'd probably be counting. I am *such* a chicken.

Dad smiles warmly. "I do remember that. Inez's story was so sad that I couldn't help but include her in the first book."

"Sad?" Sam chimes in. "Don't you mean scary? Isn't her grave part of your Graceland Cemetery tour?"

"Of course! Inez's grave is famous; hers is one of the most well-known ghost legends in the Midwest."

Mom lays a hand on top of Dad's. "I always did love the chapter you wrote about Inez. It was sad, but you told the truth—something everyone else had forgotten. It's a good life lesson, right, kiddos? Look for the story history *doesn't* tell, because that might be the one that matters!"

Aha. I see where she's going with this. Dad rarely has an agenda when we talk—it's usually just him rambling on about ghosts and graveyards and me saying "mm-hmm" over and over while I try to block out the scary stuff. But not Mom. She's always looking for "teachable moments." Sam says we should just be grateful she hasn't signed up to be a substitute teacher for our school district yet. Talk about awkward.

Clearing my throat, I work up the courage to ask Dad the question running on an endless loop in my brain. "So, um, do you know what the new book is going to be about?"

"I haven't decided for sure. I need to do more research, but I have a few ideas. But enough about the book. This looks incredible. Let's dig in!" Dad gleefully waves his fork around in the air. It looks like he's conducting an orchestra.

Looking down at my empty plate, I frown. I can't eat now. Not after hearing this news. I reach for the roll basket, knowing Mom is going to start asking questions if I don't eat something. It's empty. I shoot Sam a dirty look. "Seriously? You ate four rolls by yourself?"

"Five," he corrects. "Mom made an extra."

I stab at a sweet potato, my scowl deepening. I can't believe there was a time not that long ago when I thought Dad's job was awesome. I even helped Mom bake a cake for him when he sold his book. That was before, though. Once his ghosts took over our lives, took over *my* life, I changed my mind.

"Hey, it was awfully quiet upstairs. What were you two doing for so long?" Dad asks in between bites.

My mind goes blank. I've never liked lying. Not to anyone. I've also never been good at it. Something strange happens to my voice when I try to lie. And my eyes get all shifty. Oh, and I bite my lip. Yeah, I have no poker face. But something tells me Sam might have more experience in this department. I do my best to send a top-secret brain signal over to him: *HELP ME.*

"Research," Sam answers. His eyes find mine briefly.

"You were doing research together? That's nice," Mom says.

Good. She thinks we're talking about *school* research. Score! And really, it wasn't even a lie.

"Oh," Mom says suddenly, wiping the corners of her mouth with a napkin before setting it back down on her lap. "I almost forgot. I won't be home after school tomorrow, and neither will Dad. I've got to drop off some cupcakes downtown for an office party."

"And I need to get working on ideas for the new book, so I'll be at the library," Dad adds.

My heart sinks. Sam probably has hockey tomorrow after school. That leaves just me. Alone. Here in this house. With a ghost.

No, thank you.

I glance at Sam nervously. He just shakes his head and looks back down at the jumbled-up mess of food on his plate.

"No problem. I might hang out with Casley, anyway." I try to sound cool about this, but I'm not. I haven't even texted her back, so hanging out with her tomorrow definitely isn't going to happen.

"Perfect!" Mom says. "I'll be home around five thirty if traffic isn't too bad. The pot roast will be ready to go in the oven, though, so could you remember to do that?"

I nod somberly. There it is. The final nail in the coffin. If Mom leaves me responsible for starting dinner, I have to be here. In the ghost house.

Lucky me.

SEVENTEEN

I jerk awake, confused. I'm on the floor of my closet, half under the comforter and half on top of it. My eyes immediately cut through the darkness to the doorknob. It's still—no sign of rattling. But I heard it. I know I did, and I'm positive I wasn't dreaming. I touch the string tied around the knob of my closet door and trace the other end to the metal shoe rack. It's still secure. That string was my brilliant idea at bedtime last night. I was so tired and desperate to get some sleep. Unfortunately, I was also afraid. So I pulled the string from the waist of some old sweatpants and figured it might keep me safe if the black-eyed little boy decided to look for me again. Even though the doorknob is still, I think he has.

I lean in and put an ear against the wood. Just then, the *tick-tick* of something hard clicking against my door makes me jump back. It sounds like a fingernail. Or a claw. Whatever it is, it taps a few more times, then slowly begins dragging across the wood. It's a terrible sound...the *scritch scratch* of the evil thing that followed me home.

Holding my breath, I press back into the far wall of my closet.

Creak.

The sound thunders in my ears. It's close, like someone is walking around in my room. I lean forward, smashing the side of my face to the floor to look under the door. The space is too narrow to see much, except...a shadow. It's looming just on the other side of the door. Cold air drifts in, washing over my face and filling my nose with a strange smell. It reminds me of sweaty gym clothes left in the laundry basket too long. Wet and stale.

I sit up and try not to imagine the ghost boy standing on the other side of my door. His dark eyes. His dripping clothes and bloodless face. It's too much.

Another creak sounds, louder this time. My doorknob rattles, softly at first, then harder, as if whoever is on the other side is getting impatient. I mash my lips together to keep a scream from popping out. I can't do this. I don't know anything about ghosts! I don't know who this little boy is or what he wants!

I'm going to die of fright in my closet. My dirty, sock-covered closet.

Something thumps against my door. It's hard enough to rattle the clothes hangers dangling above my head, giving me an idea. Reaching up, I slowly untangle a thin metal hangar from the rack and stretch it out until it's straight. I have no idea if you can even poke a hole in a ghost, but if I have no choice, I'll try.

Carefully, with quivering fingers, I reach up and untie the string. It slips from the doorknob and flutters down to the floor. Taking a deep breath, I stand up. In one swift motion, I fling open the door and jab the hanger out like a sword.

It's empty. My room is completely empty. I stare at the darkness stretched out in front of me, my gaze sticking on a small patch of wood floor lit up by the streetlights outside. It looks wet. Crouching down, I use the flashlight on my phone to light up the spot even more. My breath catches in my throat. Footsteps. The wetness is a trail of footsteps that leads from the door of my room directly to the closet door. And the knob? It's still dripping.

He was here.

The air is colder this morning, like Mother Nature decided to take a step back from spring and replay winter. I blow a puff of air out, grimacing when it turns into a white cloud. Sam is in shorts today. What a nut.

"You look terrible. Did something happen that I don't know about?"

"Oh, nothing much. Just a ghost trying to kill me in my closet." I laugh weakly and roll my head from side to side. There's an annoying kink in my neck this morning, and as usual, I'm tired. More tired than I was yesterday, and that's saying something. I tried to fall asleep after discovering the watery footprints, I really did, but it just wasn't happening. I kept staring at the sweatpants string I retied to the doorknob and wondering if anything I could do would *actually* stop a ghost. I didn't think so. Once my thoughts drifted to the writing on the bathroom wall, I knew there was no point in even trying to rest. The scribbly 396 danced behind my lids every time I shut my eyes, taunting me. I'd give anything to know what it means.

I look up. Sam has stopped walking. His mouth is hanging open.

"Did you just say the ghost tried to kill you last night?" he asks.

My legs feel shaky even talking about it. "Yeah. I almost came to get you, but..."

"But what?" he presses.

"I was too scared," I admit. "It was horrible, Sam. Worse

than the wind in the living room, the wet clothes, *and* the writing on the bathroom wall. The ghost was in my room."

Sam scrubs a hand down his face. "You saw him this time?"

"No. I saw his shadow. It was underneath the closet door. Then he started rattling the doorknob again."

Things grow silent between us. Sometimes when Sam doesn't know what to say, he does this. I wish he had something to say. An idea or a plan. Anything to make this situation less scary.

"That's two nights he's come into my room. I told you, he's after me."

"I didn't know," he finally says. "I fell asleep with my headphones on. Probably wouldn't have heard it if the ghost had broken down my door." Turning to face me, his expression brightens a little. "It sucks that happened, but did he leave any clues? Anything we can use?"

I shake my head, sharp talons of fear digging into me all over again. "He didn't write anything on my wall, if that's what you mean. He just...I don't know. Terrorized me?"

"I'm sorry. We'll fix this, okay?" Sam says, giving my shoulder a few awkward pats. "It's just going to take some time."

Time I might not have, I think to myself.

EIGHTEEN

The hallway is crowded already. I duck and weave through curtains of students, sighing gratefully when I finally reach my locker. There's a cluster of people around it. A cluster of very *familiar* people. Uh-oh. I spin on my heel to go the other direction, stopping when Casley belts out my name.

"Claire. Elizabeth. Koster."

Did she just use my full name? The full name no one else even knows?

I freeze like a deer caught in headlights. The hallway has gone silent. A few giggles erupt behind me. l consider pretending I didn't hear her. Warner Jameson's locker is only five down from mine, and he's there, watching. Why me? That's a question I seem to be asking a lot these days.

"Hey, Cas," I say in the most cheerful voice I can muster.

It's hard, considering Emily is at her side again. She's like the mosquitoes that harass me every summer when we vacation in Wisconsin. Always there. Always annoying. Never helpful.

"Hey yourself," Casley answers. Today, both of them have on pale pink lipstick. "Where have you been? I've texted you like a hundred times!"

I look around awkwardly. Most of the people in the hall have gone back to their own business. The hum of conversation and the squeak of locker doors fill the dead air again. I can't feel eyes burning holes in my head anymore, either. Except for Warner's. He's still at his locker, stealing glances my way every minute or so.

Go to first period already!

"You did?" I ask nervously.

Casley narrows her eyes at me. She whispers something to Emily, who reluctantly shuffles away. "I know you saw the texts, Claire. They say 'read' on them. *All* of them."

Stupid technology. Can't a girl even read texts without people knowing these days?

"Seriously. What is going on with you?" Casley demands. "You've been grumpy since last weekend, and, well...I'm worried about you." Her eyes aren't angry or even confused. They're pleading.

"After the whole cafeteria thing," she continues, "I knew

something was wrong for sure. It's not like you to get that mad, you know? You kind of...exploded."

"Mm-hmm." Maybe if I just keep saying *mm-hmm* like I do with Dad, she'll let it go and we can just forget about what happened in the cafeteria. Then again, Casley doesn't give up easily. Probably a good thing, because her parents' divorce has put her through a lot this year.

"Claire!" She gives my shoulder a little shake. "Talk to me!"

Warner closes his locker door with a bang, making me jump. He meets my eyes for a second, then mouths "Sorry" before walking away. Sorry for what? For scaring me with his locker door, or for the angry friend questioning me right now? Maybe he's just sorry because every time we run into each other, I look more pathetic. My cheeks burn hotter than the Iroquois Theater fire.

"Listen," I say, trying to keep my voice calm and under control. *No tears. No tears. No tears.* I repeat it like a mantra. Then I lower my voice and look her straight in the eyes. "It's nice that you're worried, but embarrassing me in front of half of the school isn't really making it any better."

"Yeah, well, ignoring me isn't making it any better, either," Cas retorts. "I was afraid that if I *didn't* make a scene, you'd just walk away from me. You've been good at that lately."

Ouch. That stings. I have been avoiding Casley, but she's been avoiding me, too! Actually, she's been *ignoring* me. Big difference.

"I'm sorry." I look down at the worn tiles beneath my feet and try to think of a way to explain this to her that she'll understand. It's hard, though. Secrets suck. "I want to tell you what's going on, but I can't."

Casley looks disappointed. I feel terrible. I wish this ghost knew he wasn't hurting just me. Maybe he'd stop. Then again, maybe he's so angry about whatever happened to him that he doesn't care.

"I don't get it. Why? Why can't you tell me?" She pauses, her eyes roaming over me as if the answer might be written on my clothing or in my expression. "Does it have something to do with Emily?"

"Yes. No! Sort of." I'm digging myself into a hole I'll never get out of. Casley could help me solve this mystery, but she'd also tell Emily. Emily would tell other people. Other people would gossip, and before I knew it, my life at school would be just as miserable as my life at home. "I just can't. I'm sorry."

Cas reaches up and tightens her perfectly sleek ponytail, then sighs. It sounds irritated. "She's not how you think she is. She's really nice, Claire. You'd like her if you gave her a chance."

A tight laugh escapes me. I *did* give Emily a chance,

and all she gave me in return was lipstick. Oh, and a terrible weekend alone. "I don't trust her, Cas. I'm sorry."

Casley looks crestfallen. "Don't you trust me?"

I don't know how to answer this. I've always trusted Casley with everything, but that was before. Before the makeup, the hair, the clothes. Before Emily. Now? I'm not sure.

Her eyes grow shiny. She bites her bottom lip. "Whatever. I can't make you talk, but promise me you'll tell *someone* what's going on, Claire. Even if it isn't me. It isn't safe to keep big problems to yourself."

"I told Sam."

She stares at me like I'm speaking Japanese. "Sam. You told Sam and you won't tell me?"

I shrug. It might not make sense to her now, but if I'm lucky, someday she'll understand.

"I guess I'll leave you alone, then." Cas says, her face slack with disappointment. "But if you change your mind, I'm here."

Her voice cracks a little when she says this. I think Casley is trying to act mature even though she's hurt. I wish I could tell her I'm sorry, that I'm not keeping this secret to be mean. I'm keeping it because I don't have a choice. Right now, school is my haven. It's the only place I can escape the nightmare waiting for me at home. If I tell Cas what's happening, she'll want to talk about it and I really, *really* don't.

The bell rings, signaling that we're both about to be late to class. Casley looks down at the stack of books in her hands, then back up at me. Her eyes are glassy, like she's about to cry.

"Things change, Claire. It isn't a bad thing." Her lip trembles.

It is if you liked the way things were before.

I slam my locker closed, then do the hardest thing I've done in my entire life. Harder than going on the ghost bus. Harder than acing my last science exam. Harder even than sleeping in a dark closet every night.

I watch my best friend walk away.

NINETEEN

I'm so tired in science that I doze off. Twice. Once I catch my head just before it bashes into my textbook, and the second time, Vanessa Jacobs pokes me. Not only do I miss talking about microorganisms, but I also made myself look like an idiot.

I raise my hand. "Can I use the restroom?"

Ms. Mancini nods. Just before I reach the door, she catches up with me and taps my shoulder. "You might want to splash some water on your face to wake yourself up, dear," she whispers, smiling gently.

Nodding, I do my best to send her a silent thank-you. I love Ms. Mancini. She's the only teacher I have who wouldn't shame a student for falling asleep in class. I think she remembers what it was like to be in seventh grade and that's what makes her so good at her job.

The hallways are empty. Everyone is tucked into third period, probably fighting off either sleep or a growling stomach. I shove the bathroom door open and immediately bend down to peer beneath the stalls. I don't know why I do this every time I go into public bathrooms. I only know I can't help it. I need to know who else is in the bathroom with me, or it freaks me out when they appear. I check under all four doors. Empty.

Walking over to the sinks, I turn the cold water on. I splash my face several times, then look at my reflection in the mirror. I look terrible. My curls are kinks, my face is pale, and the dark shadows under my eyes are even worse than they were yesterday. I swear, if this ghost doesn't kill me with fright, he'll kill me with exhaustion for sure.

I'm poking at the puffy circles under my eyes when I hear the lid of a toilet drop. I'd know that sound anywhere. Sam can't seem to lower the toilet lid at home quietly, and since the bathroom shares a wall with my bedroom, the sound scares me at least twice a week. My finger is still beneath my eye, but I don't dare move. I checked every stall, and there were no legs. No feet. Nothing.

I wait for the flush, but one doesn't come. Slowly, I bend down and force myself to double-check the stalls. If someone is in here and trying to scare me, they better show themselves. Now!

First stall...empty.

Second stall...empty.

Third stall...empty.

Fourth stall...one black shoe slowly lowers to the floor. Then another. The legs attached are dressed in pants I'd recognize anywhere: knickerbockers. White knickerbockers.

I scream. The lights go out, and I'm trapped in the pitch black. I put my shaking palms on the wall. Maybe I can feel my way to the door. The wall is nothing but a bunch of square tiles, three mirrors, three sinks, and a light switch. So why can't I find the light switch?

A whispering builds from somewhere in the darkness. I stop moving along the wall.

Where are they?

Where are they?

WHERE ARE THEY?

The lights flicker on for a brief second, illuminating a face in the mirror. A bloodless face with black eyes. The bathroom is plunged back into darkness, leaving me to wonder if the boy is creeping closer, if he'll grab me any minute.

Giving up on escape, I slide down the wall onto the floor, then pull my knees up to my chin. I drop my face down onto them, cover my head with my hands, and cry. I was wrong. School isn't my haven. It isn't a safe place at all.

There are no safe places for me anymore.

TWENTY

I don't know how long I stay balled up on the floor. My tears are coming so fast and hard that they soak through my jeans. I'm hiccupping now, and any second, I just know I'm going to feel the icy cold hands of the ghost on me.

But I don't. I feel warm hands.

"Claire! Oh my god, are you okay?" The ghost sounds like Casley.

Wait, the ghost sounds like Casley? I slowly lift my head and open my eyes. The light is back on. Casley is hunched over in front of me. Her face is an ashen-white mask of fright.

"He was here," I choke out.

"Who?"

"The ghost." Just saying the words fills me with shame. I never wanted her to know about this. I never wanted anyone but Sam to know. But now the ghost has gotten into my room. My school. My *head*. I need help.

Casley gasps. She puts her hands out and helps me to my feet. I crouch down to look beneath the stalls again. All empty. Even stall number four.

"I'm so sorry," I squeak out. "I was trying to handle this on my own, but then he showed up at school and ruined my stupid haven!"

"Your what?"

I wave off her question, then fight off another round of tears. "I saw him in here. I did!"

Wordlessly, Casley double-checks the stalls. When she's finally satisfied that there's no one in any of them, she spins around to face me.

"You said *ghost*," she starts, her voice gentle. "But you don't believe in ghosts."

"I *didn't* believe in ghosts," I sniffle. "Until Saturday night."

Casley's eyebrows jump up. "Sam was telling the truth. About you going on your dad's bus."

Her tone isn't mean or even judgmental. It's disappointed. Suddenly I feel guilty for lying to her all over again.

"Yes," I say. "Dad's driver got sick, and I had to help him for a night." I decide to stop there. I've already said too much.

Casley is quiet for a few long moments. When she finally starts speaking, her expression is sad. "Remember how scared I was to tell you my parents were getting a divorce last year?"

"Yes," I whisper. The day Casley broke down and told me her parents had been fighting for months was one of the hardest days of my life. She was terrified, and all I could do was hug her. As much as I wanted one, there was no magical fix for the pain she was in. In the end, we huddled together in my room until she got tired and fell asleep, her face wet with tears. I didn't solve her problems, but I was there for her. I've always been there for her.

"It was so horrible, and at the time, it seemed like if I told anyone, even you, it was like admitting it was actually happening. I didn't want to admit that. I wanted things to stay the same." She takes a deep breath, then reaches out and gives my hand a squeeze. "I was scared. It's okay to be scared. But eventually you've got to let someone help you. I'm still your friend, right?"

Wow. I said that exact same thing to her last year. Back when she finally fessed up about why she'd been so moody. It seemed so weird that she would hide her problems from me, her best friend. Now I think I get it.

"Claire?" Casley prompts again.

I look up at the ceiling while I consider how to explain.

Wads of toilet paper that were once wet cling to the cracked plaster. Taking a deep breath, I clear my mind of everything. Of the fluttering curtains, the writing on my shower wall, the broken family photograph, and my flooded dresser. I'll take care of this ghost once and for all. But first, I need to take care of myself. And my best friend.

"You're right." I take a calming breath. "I need help. I'm scared, Cas. Really scared. All this time, I thought the ghost stories my Dad tells were silly and fake. Well, guess what? They aren't! I *did* go on his ghost tour bus, and it was the worst thing I've ever done, because a ghost followed me home. A little boy."

Casley's eyes meet mine. "That's what you were talking about when I came in and you said, 'He was here'?"

Nodding, I gesture to the stall where I saw the boy's shoes. "Yeah. He was right there in that stall. I saw his shoes, then his reflection in the mirror. He wants something, and I think he's going to keep doing things to me until I give it to him."

Casley opens her mouth to speak, closes it, then opens it again. When she finally decides what to say, it's exactly what I would have said before all this unexplainable stuff started happening to me. "I don't know, Claire. This sounds kinda—"

"Unbelievable?" I finish for her. She nods. "I know. I know how it sounds. But you have to believe me. The ghost got into my room. He broke one of our picture frames, wrote on our shower wall, and filled my dresser with water!"

As if on cue, every faucet in the entire bathroom suddenly turns on. Water pours out so fast it sprays over the edges of the sinks and begins puddling on the floor. Casley screams. The sound bounces off the walls and digs painfully into my ears. I race to the closest faucet and frantically twist the knob, but it does nothing. The water continues to gush out, drenching my shoes as it splashes over the side.

A toilet flushes. Then another. The lights flicker, threatening to go off entirely again. Casley backs up against the wall and covers her ears. Her face is frozen with fear, and her lips are trembling. Seeing my best friend so afraid sparks something in me. Something raw and surprising. *Anger.*

"Stop it!" I yell. I don't even know what direction to yell in; I just know that the ghost boy is responsible for this, and I'm not going to let him scare my best friend like he's been scaring me. "Stop it right now!"

The faucets turn off. Other than the *plink, plink, plink* of the last water drops, the bathroom is quiet again. Casley slowly uncovers her ears and looks at me, wild-eyed.

"Ghost," I whisper. My legs are shaking again, and the goose bumps are back. I hate the way this stuff makes me feel, like everything is out of control and unpredictable.

When Casley finally answers, it's only one word. An acknowledgment. "*Ghost.*"

I exhale in relief. She believes me! I'm so happy I could cry.

"I'm sorry I didn't believe you right away," Cas says, hugging me.

"It's okay. I wouldn't have, either." I laugh feebly.

She pulls back and holds me at arm's length. "How can I help?"

I swipe at my damp cheeks again. "Really? After what a jerk I've been?"

"Seriously, Claire? You're my best friend. Of course I'm going to help you. But first you have to tell me the truth about what happened in the cafeteria. The freak-out, I mean. It was about Emily, wasn't it?"

I bob my head up and down. The guilt over how I've acted since Emily came into the picture is bad, like grape-juice-on-the-carpet bad. I've been trying to tell myself that I gave her a chance, but it's totally untrue. I don't know anything about Emily. Judging her for being into makeup and clothes wasn't cool of me. Mom's teachable moments get on my nerves sometimes, but they've definitely taught me that girls can like anything they want. Nothing matters except what's inside your head. Well, and your heart. I guess that's the most important.

"I shouldn't have been such a jerk. I'm sorry." I sniffle, then swipe at my damp face with the back of my hand. "I was jealous."

"I know."

"I thought you were replacing me."

Her seal laugh breaks free, filling the bathroom with the sound of something other than the pathetic dripping of leaky faucets. Casley waves off the thought like a gnat. "Yeah, well, you're not replaceable. You're like a red Starburst, you know? No other candy will do."

I laugh at this. Casley loves her Starburst. She always claims that the red ones have a tough job, making up for all the nasty orange and yellow ones. The fact that she compared me to her favorite candy probably shouldn't make me feel so mushy, but it does.

"I'll give her a chance from now on," I promise. "A *real* one."

Casley doesn't ask who I'm talking about. She knows. "Thank you."

"You think she'll even talk to me after I yelled at her in the cafeteria?" I ask, bracing myself for her answer. If I were in Emily's shoes, I'm not sure I'd give me a second chance. "I haven't exactly been nice to her so far."

Cas nudges me playfully. "No, you haven't. But I told her

that isn't the real you. That the real Claire isn't into makeup, but she's kind and brave and an awesome friend. Trust me, that matters more to Emily than whether or not you like metallic lip gloss."

Gratitude surges through me. Even when I was being a raging jerk, Casley defended me. She really is the best.

Walking over to the silver dispenser on the wall, Cas tugs out a wad of paper towels. Handing the stack to me, she points at my face. "Here. You can't go back to class like that. You're dripping wet."

I am. I mop myself off as best I can and toss the paper towels into the trash. My wet shoes are a different story, though. No amount of paper towels is going to fix them. Guess I'll change into my gym shoes after this.

"So, what now?" I ask as we head to the door.

She grins and flings the door open. "Now we get rid of this jerk-face ghost!"

"*We?*" I ask.

Casley links her pinky with mine and lifts them in the air. "Yeah, *we*. From now on, it's always *we*. And don't you forget it, Starburst!"

TWENTY-ONE

The final bell rings exactly four hours and one minute later. I know because I watch the clock. All. Stinking. Day. I made plans with Cas to meet up on the front steps as soon as school gets out. We're going to go over everything Sam and I know about the ghost so far. Sadly, it isn't much.

Cas is already there when I walk out the doors. The breeze is still cold and wet, smacking me in the face like a damp dish towel. Blah. I can't wait for summer.

"Hey." I sit down on the step next to her. It's freezing. My poor butt is going to be numb in minutes.

"Hey," she says back, bumping her shoulder into mine. "You okay?"

"Better now. Thank you."

She smiles, her pink lipstick almost completely faded away now. "You're welcome. You ready to do this?"

"I guess so. The real question is, are *you*?" I watch her face carefully, waiting for even the smallest sign that she's afraid. Mom once said Casley was an open book. I asked her what that meant, and she told me that some people's emotions are easier to read than others because they don't try to hide anything. If Cas is scared about doing this, I should be able to tell.

"This is going to be scary, Cas, and I can't promise you something bad won't happen."

"Pffft. Stop. I'm not going to let my best friend face a ghost on her own."

Nothing. No random blinking. No squinty eyes or worried lines. If Cas is hesitant to face this ghost with me, she sure doesn't look it.

A car horn sounds in the circle drive, and I glance up to see Emily waving from a Jeep that is pulling up to the building. "School just let out. Isn't she going the wrong way?"

"She had an orthodontist appointment," Casley says. "I think she missed fifth and sixth periods."

"Oh." She must be coming back to school to get homework, or maybe she left something in her locker.

Emily climbs out of the Jeep and jogs over to us. She waves a wrinkled-up brown paper bag in the air, beaming. "I brought surprises."

I swivel around to look at Casley. "Cas?"

She puts both hands up in the air, palms facing me. "You said you were going to give her a chance, and I thought this was as good a time as any."

I did say I'd give Emily a chance, but *now*? "I just wish you had asked me, or at least given me a heads-up."

Apparently I look worried, because a flicker of sympathy flashes across Emily's face. "If it's a problem, I don't have to go."

Sighing, I shake my head. "It's not you. It's just that this is kind of a weird time."

"You need help, Claire." Casley says, staring at me pointedly. "And Emily is awesome at solving mysteries."

My eyes skip to Emily. A delicate smile fills out her face as she shrugs. "I like solving puzzles and riddles and stuff. I'm not, like, Sherlock Holmes or anything."

Casley snorts. "Whatever. You've kicked my butt at Clue like ten times now!" She leans in and whispers loudly enough for Emily to hear: "Seriously, she's vicious. Starts rumors about suspects just to throw other players off!"

I let out a snort. Emily folds her arms over her chest in mock offense, and Casley starts laughing like a loon.

Our laughter dies down, and the smile slides off Emily's face. "Look, I get how this looks, like Casley is always ditching you for me. But that's not how it is. She *wants* you to hang out with us. She says that all the time! But she also says you're stubborn and that if you don't want to, she can't make you."

I whirl around to face Casley. "You said that? That I'm stubborn?"

She plants her hands on her hips. "You *are* stubborn! As a goat!"

Emily sighs and pinches the bridge of her nose. "This is all my fault."

"It's not," Casley starts, but Emily is shaking her head.

"It is. I'd be mad, too." Emily says earnestly, tucking a chunk of hair behind her ear. "If my best friend back in Boston suddenly started hanging out with some other girl all the time, I'd feel..."

"Left out," I finish for her, remembering all the times I've felt alone because of her. "But that still doesn't mean I should have acted the way I did. I'm sorry."

Emily nods sadly. "It's okay. I didn't mean to make you feel left out. Casley just kind of appeared one day when I needed a friend. But I wasn't trying to take her from you. I swear." She sighs deeply. "Are you good at keeping secrets?"

I can't imagine what kinds of secrets a girl like Emily could have, but I perk up anyway. Knowing something—*anything*—about her (besides the fact that she loves makeup and uses a gross amount of ketchup on her fries at lunch) would make Emily a little less mysterious. It's like research. Each time you learn something new, a piece of the bigger puzzle clicks into place. Right now, the puzzle of Emily is all torn up and missing pieces.

"You have no idea," I laugh, thinking of all the secrets I've been trying to juggle.

She nods slowly, then takes a deep breath. Meanwhile, Casley looks nervous. I look back and forth between the two of them, wondering if the secret Emily mentioned is more serious than a discontinued lipstick color or mascara that smudges.

Emily blows out the breath she's been holding and meets my eyes. "Okay. Six months ago, my parents got divorced. Then my mom lost her job, and we couldn't pay our rent. That's why we ended up here."

TWENTY-TWO

I can't help it—I gasp. This is *not* what I was expecting. Not even a little.

"That's how I met Casley. I was in the locker room crying, and she heard me. Up until then, no one here had any idea what was going on or why we moved here. I didn't want people talking about us. But keeping the secret—pretending I was okay when I wasn't—was killing me. So I broke down and told Casley."

"And you found out she went through the same thing," I say, remembering how sad Casley was when her parents got divorced. It changed everything for her. Every weekend, every school event, every holiday. From that point on, she was tossed back and forth between her mom and dad, and I know it hurt, especially since they wouldn't even talk to each other.

"Yeah. I didn't expect that. But...I needed it, I guess?" She looks down at her feet, then drags her eyes back up to me. They're brimming with tears. "Casley gets it. It was great to talk to someone who understands what I'm going through."

My insides wilt at the sadness in her voice. "I'm sorry, Emily. Are things getting any better?"

Her shoulders jump slightly. "A little. Mom is talking about it more, at least. But she still doesn't have a job. We moved here to live with my uncle Brad and aunt Chrissy, and that's been okay, I guess."

"Do you miss your dad?" Maybe I shouldn't ask this. I don't want to be nosy, but I do want Emily to know I can be a good listener and, if she lets me, a good friend.

"Yes. So much." She looks back down again, the tears in her eyes finally slipping down her cheeks. "He's staying in Boston for now."

I think about all the times I've seen Emily over the past three months. I imagined that she had a perfect life at home. Perfect bedroom to go with her perfect hair and makeup. Perfect parents and perfect report cards. I even envied her perfect teeth! How could I have been so wrong?

"I didn't know. You always seem so happy."

She smiles faintly. "I was angry for a long time. But it just made things worse, so I decided to be positive." She flicks a hand toward Casley. "Casley keeps things fun. She doesn't let me think too long about the bad stuff."

And now it all makes sense. Emily doesn't bring makeup and clothes to school because she's shallow; she does it to keep things positive. Happy. And Casley wasn't trying to be popular or move on without me. She was helping her new friend the exact same way she's helped me a dozen times before—including last year when the séance rumor hit. Except unlike Emily, I haven't tried to stay positive. I've been resentful. Angry. *Wrong.*

I feel terrible.

"So that's what the makeup is all about," I say sheepishly. "I thought you were just *really* into how you look. Not that anything is wrong with that. I mean...ugh. I'm going to stop talking now."

Emily laughs, then extends her hand to reveal a tube of lipstick. It's the Déjà Vu color they were all testing at lunch the day I freaked out. "Mom lost her job, but I still have all the samples she used to bring me. Lipstick is fun. It's just color in a tube, but it can make you feel like someone else. Someone with fewer problems. I don't know. It probably sounds dumb."

"Not at all. So, is that why you dumped all that stuff out in the cafeteria the day I got so mad?" I ask. "You were trying to be positive...for *me*?"

"Yeah. You looked so upset. I thought maybe I could take your mind off whatever was bothering you."

This time I don't say something snarky or storm away. I gratefully take the lipstick from her hand and swipe a very light layer over my lips. Casley was right. Emily isn't who I thought she was.

"I didn't explain all of this to you because it wasn't my secret to share. I figured if Emily wanted you to know, she'd tell you herself," Casley says.

"So, does that mean you didn't tell Emily about my... *problem*?" I ask.

Emily snorts playfully. "She told me we were getting hot chocolate."

"I couldn't think of anything else," Casley says, laughing weakly. "I'm sorry, Claire. I was trying to be a good friend to both of you, and I guess it was harder than I thought."

"This isn't your fault. It's mine." Looking from her to Emily, I shake my head. "I'm so sorry, guys. Do you accept my apology?" I ask.

Emily grins. "That depends. Do you accept *mine*?"

"Totally." For the first time in weeks, I feel good. Like a weight has been lifted off my chest. I still have a ghost after me, but at least I have my best friend back. Oh, and a new one, too.

"All right. All right. Enough of the mushy stuff, guys! We've got a lot to do, and I have to be home by dinnertime." Casley leans over and tries to peek inside Emily's paper bag, but Emily snaps it shut.

"Uh-uh. No peeking. No, you've got to close your eyes. Both of you." Her honey-brown eyes twinkle with anticipation.

Our groans rise above the clatter of traffic in the street. Still, we do what she asks.

"Okay! Open 'em!" Emily says.

When my eyelids snap back up, I cover my mouth with freezing fingers. "Whoa. That's a *lot* of candy."

It isn't a lot of candy; it's *all* the candy. Twizzlers, Tootsie Rolls, Starburst, and Nerds. There's even some Snickers sprinkled in.

"Twizzlers are my favorite," I tell her. "But fair warning: Don't get your hands near Cas when there are Starburst involved. You might lose a finger."

Casley mimes chomping at our hands, and we laugh.

"Um...not to ruin the mood or anything, but I'm f-f-freezing." Emily says, her teeth chattering together in between words. "You guys wanna walk somewhere warmer?"

"Totally. We're definitely not lacking in the sugar department, but if you still want hot chocolate, it's my treat!" I peel my numb butt off the step, then head for the street. "Oh, and by the way—Casley brought you here so you can help us figure out who is haunting me."

I probably shouldn't have just sprung this on her, but it seems like one of those Band-Aid situations. Sometimes the faster you get something over with, the less painful it is.

"Haunting you?" Emily repeats. "Are you being serious?"

"Deadly," I say darkly. "I'm being haunted. The ghost has been in my room *and* at school."

Casley puts a hand on her shoulder. "If you're having second thoughts, it's okay. You don't have to help. It might be scary, and you've got enough to worry about right now."

Crickets. No gasps, no *seriously?* No response at all.

Suddenly, Emily starts laughing. She doubles over and slaps the tops of her legs. "Wow. You guys really had me going there for a second. A ghost? Hilarious!"

I look at Casley, then back to Emily. I shake my head somberly, hoping she realizes this isn't a joke. Understanding slowly dawns on her.

"Wow. Um, okay. Guess it's my turn to be surprised, huh?" Emily asks.

"I'm sorry," I tell her. "I feel like we ambushed you."

"No, it's okay. I'm up for helping; I'm just surprised. Are you 100 percent sure you're being haunted? I've watched a lot of those ghost shows where they investigate paranormal things, and usually there's another explanation." Her face lights up. "Ooh! Maybe you have bad pipes in your walls and they're making weird sounds! That was on one episode."

She's so excited that I hate to tell her the truth—that nothing can explain what has happened to me *except* a ghost. I've felt him, seen him, and experienced his anger for three days now.

"It's not pipes. It's a ghost," Casley says. "Claire is a great scientist, so she's already tested this theory several times." She reaches out and squeezes my hand.

"I haven't had a choice. The ghost won't leave me alone, so, yeah," I say grimly. "The theory has *definitely* been tested."

"Oh, and there's the stuff that happened when we were in the school bathroom today. All the sinks turned on, and all the toilets flushed at the same time!"

Emily's eyes widen. She purses her lips together for a moment, then gives me a half smile. "I don't know what I can do, but I'm up for trying."

Casley's face wrinkles up in concern. "You sure?"

"Why not? It sounds better than a normal school night at my house."

I smile. No wonder Casley likes Emily. She's pretty great.

Casley is laughing. She meets my eyes, obviously pleased that Emily and I are getting along.

A chill racks my body, bringing me back to the present. The *ghost*. As much fun as I'm having right now, the minute I go home, everything will go back to how it was. I've got to figure out who he is and what he wants from me.

"So, are we headed to the coffee shop, or somewhere else?" I start. "I've got about two minutes before hypothermia sets in."

"Coffee shops aren't very private," Emily offers. "I mean, for brainstorming. I'd take you to my place, but Mom isn't always up for visitors. She's still feeling pretty down about everything."

An idea forms in my sluggish brain. Maybe the best way to take Emily's mind off her problems is to distract her. My muscles clench as I consider doing the one thing I never do—letting Emily see my house. My dad's enormous ghost book collection. *My problems*.

Before I can change my mind, I clap my hands. "Let's go to my house."

Casley's head swivels back to me. Her expression is wary. At first, I think it's because she's freaked out about going to the house I just told her is haunted, but then I realize that's not it at all. She's worried for me. About *me*. Probably because I never invite anyone but her to my house. I haven't since Dad started the Spirits tours.

"No one is home," I assure her. "We'll have the whole place to ourselves."

She lifts an eyebrow and slings her bag back onto her back. "All righty, then. Your house it is."

I know I should move, but something is stopping me. Maybe it's the idea of actually finding out who this ghost is. I should want to know, right? Then I could figure out what he wants and hopefully send him away for good. I could go in the bathroom without trembling, say goodbye to my closet bed, and hang out in my room without shaking.

"Claire?" Casley nudges me with her elbow. "Did you hear me?"

I heard her, all right. I just hope the ghost didn't. No matter how brave I try to be, in the end I'm just...not. No one likes facing scary things. And this ghost is as scary as it gets.

TWENTY-THREE

It only takes us fifteen minutes to walk to my house, including a stop at Peet's for hot chocolate. It was warm and foamy and pretty much perfect for a cold spring day.

"Just throw your stuff anywhere," I say, kicking open the door of our apartment.

"Your house is so cute!" Emily says. She walks around the edge of the room, wistfully trailing a finger over the furniture. "My aunt and uncle's house is nice, but I miss having my own room. Mom gets their guest room, so I'm sleeping on a pull-out couch in the living room."

"I'm sorry. That sucks." I don't know what else to say. It *does* suck. Sometimes I complain about how cluttered and messy our house is, but at least I have my own room. Living in her aunt's house probably just reminds Emily of the divorce and all the things she's lost.

Emily stops by my dad's office door. "What's this room?"

"Nothing," I say quickly. Too quickly. Her eyebrow shoots up. "I mean, it's just my dad's office. Nothing exciting in there unless you really happen to love Post-it Notes and piles of paper."

"Sounds like a blast," Emily says with a chuckle.

"I've got to go throw something in the oven. Be back in a second." I hustle into the kitchen, where I find a tinfoil-covered pan and a small note.

Put this in the oven at 350 degrees as soon as you get home. Remember to turn it after about half an hour or it will cook unevenly. Darn hot spot! Thanks, and love you!

—Mom

I laugh at Mom's note, imagining the look she gets on her face when she talks about the dreaded hot spot in the oven. Guess it's a nightmare for a professional cook to have an oven that doesn't cook evenly. Opening the door, I slide the roast in and turn the knob to 350. Then I head back into the living room.

Casley has settled into an armchair. She's fidgety, sliding her bracelets up and down and up and down. Leaning forward, she puts her elbows on her knees as if she's waiting for me to give a speech. "Okay, time to get down to business. Start at the beginning. Tell us everything that's happened so far. We can't help you if we don't know what's going on, so don't leave anything out, even if it's scary."

I love that Cas is being so brave, but the poor girl has no idea what she's in for. Theater fires. Devil babies. Death, death, and more death. This is gonna be ugly.

Since it would take forever to tell them everything, I settle for what our English teacher would call an abbreviated version. I tell them about my parents forcing me to work on the ghost tour bus, about the Alley of Death, Hull-House, and the Couch Tomb. Then I tell them about the boy.

Casley clicks her tongue like she's considering something. "A boy, huh? Anything special about him, like a scar or something?"

Emily's face lights up. "Oh, good thinking! We can definitely figure out who the ghost is if there's something like that to go on."

"Nope," I say. "There's nothing special that I can think of. The only unique thing about him at all was his pants. They were these really old suit pants. Knickerbockers."

Emily hoots. "*Knickerbockers?* That's the stupidest name I've ever heard."

"I know!" I snag my mom's laptop from the table in the corner. As long as I don't delete any of her recipe folders or mess with any of her order forms, she won't care if I use it. Scrolling through the pictures, I magnify one that's good, then turn the screen so everyone can see it. "And they look even dumber than they sound. They're kind of like capris for boys, but sometimes they wore these tall socks under them. Anyway, those pants make Sam and me think he died in the early 1900s."

Emily stretches her arms high above her head, then yawns. She settles deeper into the couch like she's two seconds away from a nap.

Casley slides a worn notebook out of her backpack and starts scribbling out notes for herself. She's going to make a great scientist someday. "Knickerbockers. Boy. Early 1900s. Anything else?"

"Write down the number three hundred and ninety-six." I steel myself to think about that faded piece of paper again. The dark feeling that clawed around inside me when I found it, and the fear of seeing it scrawled on my shower wall. "It's important, but Sam and I haven't figured out how yet. And trust me, we researched for *hours*. Whatever that number means, it's not a simple clue."

"Three hundred and ninety-six, three hundred and

ninety-six..." Emily chants. "Could it be a death toll? Like maybe there was some terrible tragedy that killed three hundred and ninety-six people?"

Casley claps. "Yes! I told you she's good at this!"

It *is* a good idea. In fact...

I jump up and sprint to my backpack. I tucked the slip of paper I found on the bus into my science textbook to keep it from getting damaged. Actually, I stuffed it in there to keep Mom and Dad from finding it. I'm still not ready to explain any of this to them. Luckily, they don't usually rummage through my backpack or go into our bathroom unless it's cleaning day, so they haven't discovered any of the evidence yet.

Yet. I've gotta figure out who this ghost is and what he wants. Like, yesterday.

Pulling the faded paper from my book, I carefully lay it on the coffee table in front of Emily and Casley. "When the boy on the bus disappeared, he left this on his seat. For me. Before we start looking up the number as a possible death toll, maybe we should take a closer look at it."

Casley goes to touch it, but Emily swats her hand away. "Don't! If he left that for Claire to find, it's evidence. You don't want to contaminate it!"

"With what?" Casley turns her hands over and over, looking at them scrupulously. "There's nothing on me!"

"Emily's right," I chime in. "There could be fibers or something on it. Maybe there's nothing, but we'll never know if we don't truly examine it." With this, I jog to the bookshelf in the corner and pull the antique microscope down. It belonged to my grandfather and has been in our living room since he died five years ago. We only have one of the eyepieces it came with, so the magnification won't be great, but it will do for now.

"Whew!" I wipe my forehead exaggeratedly as I set it down on the table. "This thing is heavy."

Emily and Casley huddle around me. I lower the stage from the lens just enough to slide the slip of paper into the metal clips that hold it in place. Then I raise the stage again, switch out the lens, and begin adjusting. The microscope might be old, but it works.

"What do you see?" Emily asks, hovering over my shoulder.

I squint harder into the eyepiece. "Nothing special. It just looks like old paper. No extra writing, no name, no details at all."

"Huh. It's a weird shape. And that hole doesn't look like an accident. I wonder what it was for?"

Pulling away from the microscope, I look at the hole Emily is talking about. It's perfect and rimmed in metal. "I think it's some kind of tag. Doesn't it look like a giant price tag?"

"Totally," Casley leans down to look at it as I gently flip it over. "Whoever wrote the number three-ninety-six on here was in a hurry, though. It's basically scribbled."

Sliding the microscope away, I sigh in frustration. "Okay, let's go back to Emily's idea about a possible tragedy with three hundred and ninety-six deaths." I snatch my mom's computer off the floor and pull up Google. "So, there were tons of accidents in Chicago in the 1900s, but I can't find any with an exact death count of three hundred and ninety-six people. Looks like it's back to square one, Ghostbusters."

Casley crosses the idea off in her notebook. The black pen looks so final. So depressing.

This ghost is gonna kill me.

TWENTY-FOUR

The sound of the lock on the front door snags my attention. I look up just in time to see Sam come in and fling his backpack into the middle of the room, followed by his jacket. He turns to close the door, suddenly realizing he isn't alone.

Sam bends down for a moment, then stands back up and lays a hand on his chest. "You guys almost gave me a heart attack. What are you doing?"

"What are *you* doing?" I ask. "I thought you had hockey."

"Canceled," he replies. "Coach got sick, and the assistant coach is out of town. What are you guys up to?"

"We're researching. Picking up where you and I left off."

He looks at Casley and Emily, confused. "Really?"

I nod. The room is silent while he considers this.

"Sooooo, I was right." He finally says, a smug grin tugging at his lips.

"About what?" Casley asks.

"Nothing," I bark, then refocus on Sam. "*Maybe*."

He narrows his eyes at me.

"Fine! You were. Enough already." I cross my arms over my chest in a huff. It's bad enough that Sam was right about how I needed to talk to Casley instead of avoiding her. Now he knows he was right, and he's going to be impossible to live with.

Sam's eyes land on Emily. Even though he's trying to hide it, I see the smile tugging at the corners of his lips. Kicking off his shoes, he gives up and grins broadly. "Great. I'm in."

"No thanks, Romeo. We're good," I tell him.

"We're not good," Casley deadpans. "Not even close."

"Haven't figured out a thing yet," Emily follows up with a cheeky grin. "Totally clueless."

Giving Casley and Emily a stern look, I hold my arm out in front of Sam, barring him from coming into the room. He presses against it, but I muscle him backward. "We have leads. It's all good."

"Aww, let him stay. We have candy!" Emily exclaims, shaking the bag in Sam's direction. There's a smudge of something on her chin now, presumably chocolate.

Sam eyes the bag, his jaw dropping. He takes a step away from my outstretched arm and levels a serious look at me. "You guys couldn't finish all that in a million years. Plus, you need me. I know what's going on. I can help."

I give up. "Fine. You can help, but only if you focus. Okay?"

"Yup." He flings himself onto the couch, nearly sending Emily off the other end. She laughs loudly, then passes the bag of candy to him.

"Should we fill Sam in on what he missed?" Casley points to the microscope.

Emily straightens up. "For sure. Even though we didn't figure out what the number three-ninety-six means, it's obviously important."

"Oh. Did you tell them about the bathroom?" Sam asks, wincing.

"Bathroom?" Casley and Emily ask in unison.

Rubbing my temples, I groan. "I forgot to mention that the paper I showed you wasn't the only time the ghost left a clue involving the number three-sixty-nine. He also wrote it on our shower wall...in Sharpie. I feel like he's getting frustrated with me. Upset because I can't figure out what he wants." I go quiet for a moment, afraid to voice what I'm thinking. "I'm scared he's going to do something really bad."

"Let's go back to the Iroquois Theater fire," my brother suggests. "So many kids died in that. I still think this boy was one of them."

"How many?" Emily prompts.

"More than two hundred," I say gravely.

Casley's eyes darken. "Two hundred? Jeez. I'm starting to think they should call this the Fiery City instead of the Windy City."

She's right. Fire has changed Chicago over the years, and not for the better. I think about all of the headstones from the original city cemetery that were burned when the Great Chicago Fire ripped through the area—lost forever. That's part of why there are bodies beneath our neighborhood now. Once the headstones were gone, city officials struggled to locate the bodies.

Emily shimmies a Tootsie Roll across her knuckles like a coin. It travels from her index finger down to her pinky before falling off and bouncing across the floor. "Did you find anything that made you think you were right? About the boy being someone who died in that fire?"

"Nope." I shake my head, frustrated that I haven't made any more progress. A good scientist keeps collecting data until she has enough to form a hypothesis. Right now, I don't have close to enough for that.

A light bulb goes off in my head. It's a memory from the bathroom at school. "Hold on—I just remembered something that might help us."

Everyone goes still.

"When the ghost first appeared on the bus, he kept mouthing something to me. I couldn't figure out what it was, though." I pause and take a deep breath. Why don't I breathe while I'm talking? "Then, when the ghost showed up in the bathroom, he said—"

"Whoa, whoa, whoa," Sam interrupts. "The ghost showed up in the bathroom? Why didn't you tell me this?"

"Sorry. I guess I just didn't have time. Everything has been so unbelievable today." I rub at my sleepy eyes, trying not to think about how scary the bathroom incident was. The faucets turning on and the toilets flushing and...the voice. "Anyway, the ghost didn't just mouth words to me today. He *said* them. In a real voice!"

Emily looks hopeful. "What? What did he say?"

"Where. Are. They," I say. Goose bumps spring up on my arms instantly.

"Wow. I wonder who he was talking about?" Sam says. Casley is perched on the edge of her chair now. Her face is so pale that her faded Déjà Vu lips look bright all over again.

I roll my shoulders. "I don't know. But I think that's what we need to find out. He's looking for someone, and I guess he believes I know how to find them."

Every cell phone in the room comes out. Sam starts talking

to Emily about the theater fire. He whispers the number 396, and she immediately starts swiping at the screen of her phone. Casley pulls one of my father's books off the shelf. My brain kicks into high gear. We're missing something now, but not for long.

Digging around in the *Spirits of Chicago* book, I sigh. There are too many ghost legends that just don't fit. The ghost clearly isn't the Woman in Red. He isn't a devil baby. He isn't old man Ira Couch. He's a little boy, but it's beginning to seem like little boy ghost legends are rare.

"Who is Resurrection Mary?" Casley asks.

Resurrection Mary. Resurrection Mary. Resurrection Mary. I remember something about that name...something Dad said during the tour. Yes! It was one of the drive-bys!

"I think I remember hearing Dad say that no one really knows who she was for sure," I answer. "I guess back in the 1930s, a legend started about a woman on Archer Avenue who flagged down drivers and asked for a ride. When the driver got close to Resurrection Cemetery, she panicked and told them to let her out. Then she vanished."

Emily grimaces. "Vanished in a cemetery? That's scary. Couldn't she choose a restaurant or something to disappear into?"

"I doubt she was concerned about haunting people *nicely*," Sam says, laughing.

"Shut up," Emily says, flinging a ball of wadded-up Starburst wrappers at him.

"It can't be Resurrection Mary, anyway," I note. "The bus didn't go anywhere near Archer Avenue."

"But didn't you tell me that you guys drove past the spot where she supposedly died?" Sam asks.

"Yeah. But we didn't stop. That was one of the drive-bys." I say, considering the possibility. "It doesn't matter anyway, because the ghost is a boy. A brown-haired boy."

An earsplitting wail interrupts us. It's loud, like an alarm. I jump up from the floor. "Oh my god. What's that?"

Sam's eyes are huge and round. They look like two shiny moons set into pale skin. "Ghost!"

We scatter. Casley rushes behind the armchair, crouching down until she's hidden from sight. Emily bolts for the front door. Sam is paralyzed, those moon eyes of his large and panicked. I run for the stairs. If this ghost is going to get wild again, I'm not going to stand here and wait for it.

TWENTY-FIVE

"Stop!" Sam's voice rises above the wailing sound.

Everyone freezes where they are: Emily's hand on the doorknob, me on the third step. Cas peeks out from behind the armchair. She looks like one of those rotating ducks in the shooting game at the arcade.

"I think it's the fire alarm!" he yells.

Fire alarm? Oh, no! The pot roast! I sprint toward the kitchen, coughing as the air grows thicker. The entire room is smoky. I throw open the back door, grab a dish towel, and start waving it around.

The alarm finally goes quiet. My ears are ringing. I gasp for air as clouds of smoke billow past me. Casley reaches into the oven with mitts on and pulls out the pan. The entire left half of the roast is charred. Stupid hot spot!

"I can't believe I forgot about that." My insides wilt. With half the roast now a shriveled, black brick, dinner is pretty much ruined.

Sam is standing in the doorway, scowling. "Mom is *not* going to be happy."

"You think?" I yell at him. My brother has a knack for saying the exact wrong thing to me sometimes.

"Hey, it's not the end of the world. I'm sure your mom has burned stuff before," Casley says in a soothing voice. "She's a professional baker. Stuff like this happens to them, too."

"Yeah, maybe just tell her we got held up after school and when we got here it was already burning?" Emily suggests. She's fanning the smoky air away from her face with an oven mitt.

I groan. More lies. Haven't I told enough of those lately? No—if Sam could find the guts to tell Mom and Dad he failed a math test, then I can tell them I burned the stupid pot roast. "It's okay. I'll just tell her what happened, that I got distracted and forgot."

"Well, whatever you decide to tell her, we don't have time to waste," Sam pipes up. "We need to finish this research. *Fast.*"

He's right. I fan the room with the dish towel one more time. "Okay, let's go."

The smoke is better in the living room. Casley sits in the chair again, her legs folded up underneath her. I take a spot on the rug with my books. My brain is spinning but going nowhere. We sit in silence for the next ten minutes, each of us lost in our own research. I press my fingers into my aching temples and rub.

It's hopeless.

Suddenly, Sam stands up. The book that was in his lap falls to the floor with a thunk. He walks to the window and looks out, then begins robotically closing each of the shades, one at a time.

"Weirdo, what are you doing?" Emily asks with a smirk.

Sam pauses at the third window. "I don't know. I just...I feel like someone is watching us, you know?"

Goosebumps rise all over my skin. I *do* know that feeling. Standing up, I stretch my arms out to my sides in a T shape. Then I wait. If I feel even one burst of wind—no matter how small—I'm outta here.

The ghostly breeze never comes. But the *feeling* does. I sink back down onto the floor and stare at the worn rug beneath me. Something is missing. But what? Is it missing for me or missing for the ghost boy?

What is missing?

"Claire?" Casley scoots over next to me, notebook in hand. "What's wrong?"

It's so hard to explain. "There's this feeling I get when

the ghost is around. It's b-b-bad," I stammer out. Wrapping my arms around myself, I try to keep my teeth from chattering. No luck. It's freezing in here. "It feels like I'm missing something, but I don't know what it is."

Emily stiffens. She tilts her head to the side. "Do you guys hear that?"

"Hear what?" Sam asks.

"That sound. It's"—she pauses, swiveling around to look at the wall behind us—"it's coming from the wall. It sounds like something scratching around in there. You don't have mice, do you?"

Oh, no. No, we don't have mice. *But we do have a ghost.*

My cell phone suddenly vibrates in my pocket. Then again and again and again. By the time I manage to fish it out, my screen is filled with the same text message over and over.

WHERE ARE THEY WHERE ARE THEY WHERE ARE THEY WHERE ARE THEY WHERE ARE THEY WHERE ARE THEY WHERE ARE THEY WHERE ARE THEY WHERE ARE THEY WHERE ARE THEY WHERE ARE THEY WHERE ARE THEY

I open the first text, gasping when I discover the number it came from is not a normal phone number at all but only three digits: 396.

Emily scrambles to her feet and covers her ears. "You guys don't hear that? It's so loud!"

Casley's eyes are so huge she looks like an owl. They dart around the room, then land on me. "No, I hear it. What's happening, Claire? Does that sound mean the ghost is here?"

I nod as my phone slips from my fingers and lands on the rug. No more secrets. The ghost *is* here. I can feel him again. A dripping sound draws my gaze to the stairwell. *Plink. Plink. Plink.* It starts out quiet—nothing more than a watery echo in the air. Then it builds. I stare in horror as a river of water begins trickling down the steps. It slithers down and puddles on the hardwood floor at the bottom.

"What is that?" Emily screams.

I snatch my books up off the floor and toss them onto the couch. Running over to the stairs, I touch a finger to the water. It's freezing. "Water. It's coming from upstairs. Sam, c'mon!"

I'm on the fourth step when I notice he's still standing in the living room. "What are you doing?" I yell. "Help me figure out where the leak is coming from before the entire house is ruined!"

Casley is beside me in a flash. Emily tugs on Sam until his feet finally start moving. Good thing, too. If Mom was going to be mad about the burned pot roast, I have no idea how she'll react to a flooded house.

Other than the sound of water dripping, the upstairs is eerily quiet. The sun is gently dipping in the sky, sending shadows dancing across the walls. The same soft whisper I heard in the bathroom at school starts up again like a chant. An eerie, warning-filled chant.

Where are they?

Where are they?

Where are they?

Sam grips the banister at the top of the stairs. His knuckles turn white. "Please tell me you guys hear that, too."

Casley nods solemnly. Emily plugs her ears.

"I'd say they hear it," I answer him.

The whispering sinks back into the walls and leaves us in silence. My heart pounds harder.

All three of them fall in line behind me. The thick, plush carpet squelches beneath my feet. Mom and Dad are going to flip when they see this.

I creep toward the bathroom, gasping when I see that the light is on and the bathtub is empty. The sink, too. "Oh, no. It's not coming from here."

Sam's face pales. "Mom and Dad's bathroom?"

I take off at a full-on sprint. Mom and Dad had their bathroom completely remodeled about a year ago. It's their pride and joy. A shower the size of Cook County, a Jacuzzi tub, gleaming marble floors, and a walk-in closet for two. It's amazing. And if I'm not wrong, it's also flooding.

Skidding to a stop, I scream as their bathroom comes into view. Water is rushing out from beneath the door. I fling it open, wincing as it cracks against the wall. The bathtub is overflowing. I slog through the water, slipping and sliding until I get to the porcelain edge. Leaning over, I twist the knobs until the water finally stops.

A horrible quiet falls over us as we look around. A half inch of water is standing on the marble tiles. The carpet outside of the bathroom is drenched. A home-decorating magazine is floating by the shower.

"Who would do this?" Casley whispers.

"The ghost, that's who!" I shout. My eyes find the bathtub again, and I gasp. It isn't filled with just water—there's paper, too. Lots of paper. The ink is running off, turning the water a murky gray. Tears prick at my eyes as I reach a hand in and grab a piece. The paper that comes out is blank, all but one word.

Eastland.

TWENTY-SIX

Every towel we own is on the floor. Hand towels, guest towels, beach towels—they're all lined up on the carpet like some kind of weird patchwork quilt. Sam is trying to reach Mom and Dad on the phone while the rest of us work to soak up the water. This is a disaster. A full-on, pack-my-things-and-move-out disaster.

I fish another wet paper out of the tub. Dad's entire stack of research is in there, ruined. This is exactly why I tell him he should use his computer instead of writing everything by hand! Stuff happens. Ghosts happen. At least they do in this house.

My legs are shaking as I take the last few sheets over to the counter and lay them out. The lone black word stares back at me from the pile of mushy white—*Eastland*. The boat that capsized in the Chicago River, killing so many people. So many *children*.

Could the ghost boy have died on the *Eastland*?

I shake my head, trying to clear the jumble of thoughts. Right now, I need to focus on how to soak up this water. Well, that and how to keep myself and Sam from getting grounded. I turn to Casley. "You guys need to get out of here."

"What? Why?" she asks. She's wringing a towel out over the sink.

"Because you have to. My parents are going to be mad when they come home, and I don't want them blaming either of you," I admit. Emily is down on her hands and knees, pressing a dry towel into the carpet of my parents' bedroom. I won't let my friends take the fall for any of this mess. Especially Emily, who doesn't need any more problems than she already has.

Casley doesn't move, so I snap a soaking-wet towel at her. It catches her on the leg with a smack. She yelps.

"I mean it, go!" I yell, flapping my hands in the air like I'm chasing away a flock of pigeons. "I'm trying to help you, trust me."

Cas shrugs and puts her towel down. "Call us if you need help, okay? This wasn't your fault. We can help you explain."

"Explain what? That a ghost is terrorizing me? My dad would *love* that, Cas. He'd go wild if I told him the truth about this." It's a horrible thought, one that fills my entire body with dread.

More research.

More scary stories.

More *ghosts*.

I blink away tears. "Thank you for everything, guys. I'll text you tonight and let you know what happens. If I still have a phone, that is."

Casley flinches and shakes her head. "You will. It's going to be all right, Claire."

After a quick hug, she walks away. I'm sitting on the floor, shivering from the cold water that has soaked through my jeans, when Emily comes into the bathroom.

"You going to be okay?" she asks. Her jeans have wet spots on both knees, and the skin of her palms is pruney.

"Yeah. I'll be fine. Sam, too."

Emily lifts her sweater sleeve and separates her dangly silver bracelets so I can see them all clearly. "These bracelets are my favorite things. I bought one on each vacation I took with my family—you know, before things changed. They remind me of good things, so I wear them all the time."

Sliding one of the bracelets off, she presses it into my hand. It has charm with a blue shark on it. "This one is from my trip to Martha's Vineyard," she says with a smile. "It's a tradition to jump off the bridge from the *Jaws* movie there, you know? I was so scared that I almost didn't do it even though I'd been looking forward to it for days. When I finally did it, I was so relieved. Proud of myself for being brave and for surviving even though it was scary."

"Are you saying that if I face the ghost, I'll be proud later?"

"I'm saying it's okay to be afraid. You'll survive anyway; I know it."

I slip the bracelet onto my wrist and smile, remembering the day Sam told me he knew about my counting habit. He said almost the exact same thing—that it's okay to be afraid. He was right. They both are. Fear can't stop me from solving this mystery unless I let it, and I'm definitely not planning on doing that.

"Thanks, Em. This means a lot." She starts to walk away, but I reach out and grab her wrist at the last second. "Hey, um...you sure *you* don't need this?"

Emily's eyes slide down to the bracelet she just gave me. The one I already love but would be willing to give back in a heartbeat if she needs it more than I do.

She gives a sad shrug. "I'm sure. Mom is strong. She'll get past this. Plus, she's got something in common with you that just might help her."

"Oh yeah? What's that?"

"She's stubborn," Emily says with a giggle. "As a goat! Pretty sure she isn't gonna stay down for long."

I shake my head, laughter tumbling from my lips. "No, she won't."

Running a finger over the bracelet, I inhale deeply. It feels good, like a reminder that even though Emily wears cool clothes and knows how to put on makeup, deep down she's no different from me. Everyone needs help sometimes, even the girls who look like they don't. Even the girls who seem perfect.

"Thanks for helping."

Emily makes a fist, holding it out in front of me like I've seen her do with Casley. "No prob. Thanks for today."

I touch my knuckles to hers, giggling. "For bringing you to my house of horrors?"

Emily's shoulders shake gently as she starts laughing. "No. I mean, thanks for letting me help. It's nice to be the one helping instead of the one needing help for once."

I smile, hoping she knows how thankful I am.

Sam walks in just after Emily leaves. His mouth curves into a lopsided smirk as he reaches for the last dry towel we could find.

"What?" I ask. "What could you possibly be smiling about right now?"

"Nothing. It's just that in a weird way, the ghost helped

you make up with Casley *and* become friends with Emily. You hated her yesterday!"

I don't miss the way his eyes light up when he mentions Emily. "I didn't hate her. I just didn't know her. And you aren't *at all* happy about knowing Emily now?"

"I didn't say that," he laughs, his cheeks staining pink.

"Mm-hmm." I look around the waterlogged room and groan. "The ghost may have pulled us all together, but he also wrecked our house."

"Think Mom and Dad are going to kill us?"

"Maybe," I say. "I mean, what are we going to tell them?"

"I've been trying to figure that out since I first saw the water on the stairs."

I stop stepping on my towel. "Sam?"

"Yeah?"

"I think the ghost boy died on the SS *Eastland*."

My brother sits back on his haunches, studying me. "I thought the bus didn't stop by the *Eastland* disaster area."

"It didn't," I respond.

"Then what makes you say that?"

I think about his question. What *is* making me say that? I review the evidence the ghost has left us. For one, the boy looked wet when I saw him. For another, he filled my dresser drawers with water, turned on the faucets in the bathroom at school, *and* just tried to drown us in our own house. Then there's the papers. The *Eastland* research.

"A lot of the hints the ghost has been leaving have to do with water. Like this," I say, lifting a soggy sheet of Dad's research. It tears in half, and part of it falls to the floor with a wet slap. "Why would these specific papers be in the tub? Why not something of yours or mine instead? And why write three-ninety-six in the shower instead of somewhere like the living room wall, where it would be more obvious?"

Sam doesn't answer, so I tell him. "Water. He's trying to tell us water is important."

My brother stares at the paper on the floor. "If you're right, then we need to find out who he was and what he wants, or we won't have a house to come home to anymore."

I look around the wet space and inhale deeply. "I know. It seems like he's angry now."

"Or maybe just scared." Sam looks up from the towel he's kneading into the carpet.

Scared. It's an emotion that everyone feels. Big, small, old, young—we all feel fear, and *if* the little boy haunting me actually died on the SS *Eastland*, then I have no doubt he was terrified. The thought makes me sad.

"LaSalle and Wacker," I announce.

"What's that? The spot where the boat sank?" he asks.

"Yup. That's where the tour bus was when Dad was giving the *Eastland* part of the talk. We need to go there. See if the ghost has left any clues. Or"—I pause mid-sentence, almost afraid to say what's on the tip of my tongue—"or if he shows up. It's time to test our hypothesis."

Sam stands and dumps his towel into the tub. It's already overflowing with at least two dozen other wet ones. "Tomorrow? After school?"

"Don't you have hockey tomorrow?"

He grumbles something under his breath as he checks his phone. "Yeah. But this is more important. This is life or death."

Life or death. The words echo in my mind. How in the world did things come to this?

TWENTY-SEVEN

"Calm down and tell us from the beginning—what *happened*?" my father says as he crosses the threshold into the kitchen. His hands are perched on his hips, and his tie is loosened around his neck. Mom is right behind him. I can tell the minute she smells the burnt post roast, because she scrunches up her face.

"The bathtub ran over," Sam says glumly. I flinch and scrape more burned bits of roast out of the pan and into the trash. "We called you guys right away and did the best we could to clean up, but it was bad."

"How bad?" Mom asks nervously.

"All the carpet upstairs is wet," I say. "There was so much water it started running down the steps." I think back on those first plinking sounds, remembering how hauntingly similar they were to the sounds in the school bathroom after the faucets turned on by themselves. Those things can't be coincidental. They just can't.

I watch Dad's face turn several shades of red as he stalks toward the living room. I feel bad. Terrible, actually. The tears fall before I can stop them. This is all my fault.

Things can't get much worse, so I decide to tell Mom about my dresser and the wet clothes. The clothes I *still* haven't done anything about. She looks at me quizzically. "What are you talking about?"

"My clothes! They're soaked and probably growing mold by now," I snap before I can stop myself. None of this is Mom's fault, and I know it. Still, I'm terrified. I'm also way too tired, and that's making everything worse.

"I did laundry before I left the house this morning, Claire, and loaded clean clothes into your dresser. There was nothing wrong with it," Mom says calmly.

"That's not possible," I say. "I saw it with my own eyes."

She shrugs. "Are you sure you didn't dream it, honey?"

I snort. You have to sleep to dream, and I haven't been doing much of that these days.

No, I didn't dream it. I didn't get overstimulated and imagine it, either. Just like I didn't imagine any of the other weird happenings around here.

"Claire! Sam! Come out here, *now*." Dad's voice jars me back to the current problem.

I follow my brother into the living room with Mom on my heels. Dad is halfway up the stairwell. The second he sees us, he shakes his head. "I just don't understand what you two were thinking."

"We didn't do this, Dad," Sam starts.

I'm prepared to do whatever it takes to keep my brother from spilling the truth, but Dad beats me to it. He holds a hand up in the air, his face stern. "I was researching, and your mother was filling an important catering order when you two called us in a panic. We dropped everything. We rushed home." He sighs and runs a hand through his disheveled hair. "Was this your attempt at some kind of belated April Fool's joke?"

"Joke?" I ask. "Why would it be a joke?"

"Because there's no water upstairs, Claire."

I can't speak. It's like my brain has stopped controlling my tongue, and all I can do is stare at my father in shock.

"No water?" Sam says, craning his neck to look up the stairwell. "Seriously? You didn't see the bathroom? And the carpet in the hall?"

"And your research papers," I add. "I laid them out on the sink to dry. The ink was running all over, and you couldn't even read them."

Dad looks at Mom, then back to us. "The carpet is dry. My papers are dry. There's nothing wrong upstairs."

I glance at the stairwell nervously. "That's not possible."

It's *not* possible. Four of us saw the water. Four of us mopped it up for more than an hour. There's no way we imagined all that.

"Stop. Just stop, Claire," Dad says, exchanging a frustrated look with Mom.

"Why would you two make up such a horrible story?" Mom asks. Suddenly, I feel like I'm in a police station, being questioned for a crime I didn't commit.

Sam is watching me carefully, probably trying to figure out what our next move should be. We only have two choices: tell the truth about the house being haunted or lie and say the whole overflowing tub thing was just a prank. It's a lose-lose situation.

When neither of us answers, Mom pinches the bridge of her nose and groans. "All right, then. Until you two are ready to talk about this, you're grounded."

Grounded? My mouth flops open. I've never been grounded. Maybe I've come close once or twice for being sarcastic, but it has never actually happened.

I shove past my mother and Sam, my heart aching like it has been slashed in two. Just when I think I'm home free, Dad catches my elbow.

"Are you sure you don't want to talk about this, Claire? About *anything*?" The anger in his eyes is gone. He looks hopeful now. It's the same look he gave me on the Spirits bus when he thought I might share details about the little boy with him. I feel my walls going up again. Being grounded is miserable, but being Dad's newest book topic would be worse. With my luck, he'd offer the ghost boy our guest room instead of helping us get rid of him.

"No," I mumble. "I'm good."

TWENTY-EIGHT

I'm huddled up in a mess of blankets and pillows when I hear my bedroom door open.

"Claire?" A whisper carries into the closet. I'd be afraid that it's the ghost boy coming to kill me, but I know better by now. He doesn't want to kill me; he just wants to ruin my life.

I open the closet door a crack. Sam is standing in the middle of my room in sweats and a Donald Duck T-shirt.

"In here," I whisper back. Flipping on my flashlight, I have to shield my eyes from the blinding beam.

"You weren't joking when you said you've been sleeping in the closet."

"Nope."

My brother eases himself into the cramped space. He looks like an origami grasshopper all folded up like that. "Why did you lie to Dad?"

"Why didn't you?" I fire back. "Were you really going to tell him our house is haunted after I asked you not to?"

Sam's face grows serious in the shadows. "Maybe. Things are getting out of control, Claire. What happened tonight was scary."

"I know. I just don't get it. When I ran up here, Dad was right. It looked like the flood had never happened."

"Did it?" Sam asks.

"Of course it did! I saw that water. *We* saw that water."

Sam nods like he agrees, but his scrunched-up eyebrows make me think he doesn't.

"What?" I ask.

Shrugging, he lowers himself down onto the floor. "I don't know. It might be nothing. I just can't stop thinking that maybe there never was any water in here. That maybe the ghost just made us think there was."

"How would he do that?"

"I don't know," Sam admits. "But I don't think that matters. If I'm right, then that would mean the ghost wants only us to know about him."

The idea sparks a memory. One time in music class, my teacher taught us about music and different sound pitches. She said there are some frequencies of sound—really high ones—that adults can't hear, but kids usually can. Could this be similar? Could the ghost be communicating with us in some way that only we can see and the grown-ups just...can't?

I think about the storm I saw after school on Monday. It was so realistic. But when Dad came home, he said it hadn't stormed. I even looked outside for myself and saw sunshine. And my dresser! Mom said there was nothing wrong with it even though I know what I saw.

"O-kay. But if you're right, why? Why wouldn't the ghost want anyone else to know he exists? If he wants something, wouldn't it make more sense for him to get as many people to help him as possible?"

My brother looks lost. "No clue. But I think that's something we need to figure out."

The scientist in me gets restless. I understand my brother's theory that the ghost is keeping himself hidden from adults, but without proof that it's correct, I can't agree. "Wait! I know. If you're right and the ghost is trying to communicate with us *and* keep Mom and Dad out of it, then the Sharpie would be gone now, too, right?"

Sam's eyes widen. "Bathroom?"

I nod and jump up. Mom and Dad never use our bathroom. In fact, a year ago they decided we should be the ones to empty the trash and clean up in there. You know, learn-to-be-mature chores. I used to complain about it, but now I think we're lucky because it means neither one of them could have discovered the Sharpie on the wall.

When Sam and I get to the bathroom, he gestures for me to pull the curtain aside.

"Why me?" I hiss.

"Because this is your ghost, not mine!"

Sighing, I hold my breath and gently slide the curtain to one end of the shower rail. *Gone.* The writing is gone. "You didn't do this?"

My brother looks lost. "Nope. Didn't have time."

"The broken frame is probably fixed, too." I scrub at my tired, stinging eyes. "This is bad, Sam. Really bad."

"Are you kidding? This is great! At least the ghost isn't *actually* destroying our house!"

"Don't you get it? This means his means he's targeting *us.* Just us. Why? What does he want from me?" I choke back a sob. "I don't know even know what's real and what's not anymore."

"Who cares if the ghost doesn't want Mom and Dad to know he exists?" Sam counters. "*You* don't want them to know, either. Aren't you and Ghostie kinda on the same page about this?"

I shake my head so hard my brain hurts. "I don't want Mom and Dad to know because I don't trust them. It's different."

"Maybe he doesn't trust them, either."

I lift my head. That's an interesting theory. But testing it is going to be hard. First, we need to know who the little boy was, and that means figuring out if we're right about him coming from the SS *Eastland*.

We sneak back down the hall to my room, then sit down on the edge of my bed. Reaching over to unplug my phone, I open the text messages. The one the ghost sent me—the WHERE ARE THEY message—is gone, too.

"The text is gone," I say, flipping the screen around so Sam can see it. He reaches out to still my shaking hand so he can see it more clearly. "There's no proof that this ghost exists at all. Nothing. It's just like every time he's come into my room—I hear him and feel him. At school I even saw him! But I can't prove that he was ever there."

"You don't have to prove it to anyone," Sam says softly. "I believe you. So do Emily and Casley."

I set my phone down and wistfully run a hand over my bed. I'd give anything to sleep here tonight, comfortable and cozy in my fluffy blanket. My eyes feel like sandpaper, and my neck is still sore from sleeping all bent up last night. It doesn't matter that the ghost isn't actually destroying our house. He's destroying me. This has to stop.

"So, what's our plan?" I ask.

My brother pulls his knees up further and leans his chin

on his forearm. In the dark and wearing that silly shirt, he looks like an eight-year-old. A giant eight-year-old, but still. "You're the one who likes to plan, not me."

"Mom and Dad are really mad. We're grounded. I know it's going to be hard, but we still need to find a way to go downtown."

Sam leans forward in anticipation. "You mean to the spot where the boat sank?"

"Yeah. We can look around. See if there are any other clues. If our hypothesis is right, I'm guessing he'll give us proof."

Sam bites his lip. He looks skeptical. "Would the ghost hang out around the spot where he died? I mean, wouldn't that be too traumatic for him, or whatever?"

"I don't know, but looking there is better than sitting around and waiting for him to leave more clues here."

"True. Let's go tomorrow after school. We need to get rid of this ghost before I get blamed for anything else and Mom and Dad decide to send me away. I would really suck at military school." With this, he salutes me crookedly, then straightens his arms and legs like a soldier. He looks ridiculous.

I can't help but laugh. Mom and Dad can get pretty upset with us sometimes, but they'd never ship one of us off to a boarding school. Even if the pot roast fiasco had burned down our entire house, they'd still love us. I know this. I just wish they trusted me. *Understood* me. Then Dad would stop forcing me to listen to his ghost stuff, and maybe, just maybe, I could tell them about the ghost boy. Maybe they'd even be able to help us solve this. Even though I'm so tired I can barely keep my eyes open, I smile at the thought.

I'm easing back onto my dirty sock pillow when a bad thought sends me bolt upright again. "Wait. We still haven't figured out how we're going to get downtown since we're grounded."

"They can't keep us from doing school stuff. We'll just have to tell them we have projects to work on after school or something," Sam says, pulling himself into a standing position.

"You mean lie." My stomach clenches up again. Haven't I lied enough lately? I hate this. Hate what the ghost boy is making me do.

"Yeah, lie. It's not like we have a choice. The ghost is getting desperate."

He's not the only one.

"So, we'll meet on the front steps of the school tomorrow afternoon. I'll text Casley and Emily tonight and tell them. They'll probably want to help. If they're not too scared after today, anyway." I walk back to my closet and pull out the pointy straightened hanger and my Louisville Slugger. "Pick one. The ghost could still come back tonight."

Sam eyes both options, finally taking the bat from my hands. Then he tosses me one final salute. It's still crooked. He really would suck at military school. "I have better aim than you. Night, dork."

I shove him away, laughing. "Night, dweeb."

TWENTY-NINE

A cloud of confusion hangs over me the entire way to school the next day. My feet keep moving forward, inching closer and closer to eight hours in chairs that make my butt go numb, but my brain drags behind. Even though it has only been four days since the ghost started haunting me, it feels like an eternity.

Slowing down to kick the wet bits of spring from my sneakers, I groan. Sam does a 180 to face me.

"What's wrong now?"

"Same thing that's been wrong since Saturday," I snap. "I hate this so much. I hate the ghost boy, but I feel bad about that. If he really is from the *Eastland* disaster, I should want to *help* him, not kill him all over again."

My brother pulls his stocking cap down farther over his

ears. "We don't have time to feel bad for the ghost right now, Claire. We don't even know who he is yet."

I know this. Really, I do. But the tiny bit of research I did on the SS *Eastland* was depressing. Scary. *Awful.* The promise of a perfect summer day gone wrong. All of the people who boarded the ship that day were promised a luxurious cruise. Sun, water, and a fancy company picnic. An afternoon they'd never forget.

Those poor people.

Pressing the school doors open, I tell myself I need to stop. Obsessing over the ghost for the next eight hours won't get me anywhere.

"Hey," Sam says, tugging me to a stop beside him. "What's up with your locker?"

"What?" I squint down the hall at my locker bank and see yellow caution tape across it. My heart sinks. "My locker! What did they do?"

"Don't know. I've never seen that before."

I whirl around and bound toward the office. There has to be a mistake. Racing through the door, I skid to a halt just before crashing into the main desk. The woman behind it looks unimpressed.

"Well, that was an entrance."

"Sorry about that. I need help with my locker."

The woman grumbles something under her breath and then turns her pale green eyes on me. "Just think for a minute, and I'm sure you'll remember it. It happens to everyone."

If a giant winged dinosaur flew into the office right now and ate my backpack, I couldn't be more irritated. "I didn't *forget* my locker combination. I can't use my locker. At all. It's, like—it's all taped up."

Suddenly, her eyes light up with recognition. "Oh, are you in the locker bank on the main floor?"

"Yes. My name is Claire Koster. Mine is the second locker from the left side, and I can't get to any of my things." I steal a glance at my phone. "I've only got ten minutes until the first bell rings."

Her eyes skim across the counter until they find what they are after—a thick binder. She opens it up and drags her index finger across rows of print. It stops on one row and taps once, twice, three times. "Yes. Here we are. It appears that your locker has been temporarily reassigned."

"Reassigned?" I squeak out. "Why? Where?"

The book closes with a thud. "The contents of your locker were relocated to the next bank because we needed to fumigate." She hands me a slip of paper.

Fumigate? "So, does that mean they sprayed for bugs or mice or something?"

She nods. "There was a report of a bug that may or may not have been a cockroach in the locker at the center of that bank, and the school can't be too careful. So, they've fumigated the entire bank. We'll let you know when it's reopened, and you can take your original locker back. Though I wouldn't expect that before next semester."

She turns to walk away, then stops as if remembering something. "Your new locker number is on that paper I gave you."

Okay, number one: a cockroach? Gross! And number two: The locker bank next to mine is where Warner's locker is. I'll be even closer to him now. My stomach twists uncomfortably. I'm not sure if this is good or bad. It's just *something*.

I wait until I am outside the office before I text Sam. Once I let him know what's going on, I unfurl the slip of paper in my hand.

Locker #396

You have got to be kidding me.

THIRTY

A deep rumble of laughter echoes down the hallway. Warner. He's standing at his locker bank—*my* locker bank, now. Five or six boys are gathered around him. They remind me of those big groups of geese down at North Pond. What do they call those things? Gaggles?

I scan the hallway for Casley, giving up when I don't see her. Emily is nowhere to be seen, either. No friends around to help me survive Warner and his gaggle. No friends to remind me that I know how to put one foot in front of the other and speak in words that aren't total gibberish. Taking a few steps closer, I swallow hard when the locker numbers become visible. My new, reassigned locker isn't just *closer* to Warner's, it's directly beside it. Of course it is. Because, *life*.

"Excuse me," I whisper. Two guys scoot to the side

enough for me to shimmy through. I spin the knob on my lock between my thumb and forefinger, paying more attention to the conversation Warner and his friends are having than my combination. *Practice has been hard. Coach has been a jerk. Running laps is the worst.* I land on the last number and give a hard downward tug, but the lock doesn't open.

The sound of my lock refusing to grant me access seems to thunder through the hall. I must look like a sixth grader, hunched over a lock, red-cheeked and embarrassed. Whoever said those humiliating days were over when we graduated to seventh grade must not know that these kinds of moments always seem to find me.

"Claire?" Warner starts. "What happened to your locker?"

"Cockroach." It's the only word that comes out of my mouth. I freeze, realizing I've just announced to half of the baseball team that there was a cockroach in my locker. Which there most definitely was not. I want to curl up and die. Actually, I just want to die. Curling up would take too long.

Warner doesn't look at me the way I expect him to, like I have a flesh-eating disease. Instead, he eyes my old locker. "Gross. They blocked off the whole bank for one stupid bug, though? Couldn't they just smash it and get it over with?"

I giggle at this. "You'd think."

He laughs with me. His voice is so different this year.

Last year he was so much shorter, and his voice was higher. It seems like everyone changed overnight. Everyone but me.

"Hey, I'll catch you guys later, okay?" Warner says to his friends. They grunt their understanding and slowly wander away. I can feel their eyes on me as they leave, though, probably wondering why their buddy is wasting time talking to me—the daughter of wacky David Koster.

Slipping his backpack onto his shoulders, Warner leans against his locker to face me. His breath smells like peppermint. "So...rough morning?"

"If by rough you mean the worst ever, then yeah." I try for a smile. It probably doesn't work. I really don't feel like smiling, even if it is at the cutest boy ever.

"Sorry." Warner reaches over and grabs my lock. "What's your combo?"

"Fourteen, nine, eight," I say, watching his fingers twist and turn the knob until it opens. "Thanks."

He shrugs. "No problem. Can't say I've had a cockroach in my locker, but someone did think it would be funny to empty an entire can of Axe body spray into my gym locker last year. Mr. Williams wouldn't let me come to class out of uniform, so I had to suck it up and wear the clothes. I reeked all afternoon."

"Gross!" I exclaim, wrinkling up my nose. "That stuff is so nasty."

"No kidding. I smelled so bad it was giving people headaches!" Warner laughs at the memory, then goes quiet. "Hey, since we're on the subject of bad mornings, I saw what happened with Casley and Emily the other day. Things looked a little awkward."

I snag two books and a folder out of my locker. Balancing them in the crook of my arm, I add my binder to the top of the pile and slam the locker door shut again. "Yeah, Casley wasn't very happy with me."

"Everything okay now?"

What a loaded question. I'm grounded. A ghost is after me. The locker of the boy I crush on every single day is now directly next to mine. Oh, and today after school, instead of playing a sport or doing homework like a normal person would, I'm going downtown to stare at the spot where a boat sank more than a hundred years ago. At least the problems between Cas and me are fixed.

"Yeah, they're better. I just didn't know Emily before. I get why Casley likes her now, though. Emily is cool."

He grins. "Whew! Would've been awkward if you'd said you hated Em or something. You know, with her being my cousin and all."

"Emily is your cousin?" I ask, stunned. "No way!"

"You didn't know that?" he asks, laughing. "I thought the

whole school knew. Emily's mom is my mom's sister." Warner's smile falters. "She, uh, she moved here to be a little closer to family, so they're staying at my house for a while."

No wonder I've seen them together so much! The couch Emily is crashing on is Warner's.

I look around to see if anyone is listening to us before leaning in. "I know why they moved here, Warner. Emily told me."

He lets out a breath. "She did?"

Nodding, I offer a sympathetic smile. "Yeah."

"Wow. Em is pretty private about all that. Doesn't want anyone feeling bad for her." He looks up and meets my eyes. "I'm surprised she told you and Casley."

"I'm not," I say. "Cas is great. She's a good listener and an even better friend. And I was kind of a jerk. Emily only told me because she had to."

Warner's mouth pulls up into a reluctant smile. "Doubtful. I've seen you be a lot of things, but a jerk isn't one of them."

Was that a compliment? My cheeks heat up. "We should all hang out sometime. I mean, if you want to."

"Cool. What about today? You doing anything after school?"

The paper with the number 396 on it is suddenly burning

a hole in my jeans pocket. "I'm busy. Sorry. This...*thing* came up last night, and I don't think I can cancel."

Warner kicks at an imaginary something on the floor with the toe of his shoe. "Bummer. I was just thinking that maybe if you haven't finished your research for that history project, we could do it together. I mean, I think we chose the same person to write about."

"You chose to write about Dexter Graves?" I didn't realize anyone even knew who Dexter Graves was except for me. Dad has blabbered on about him for years. Actually, he's blabbered on about his *grave* for years. If you believe the stories my father spins, staring into the eyes of the enormous hooded statue guarding poor Dexter's grave will give you a vision of your death. Before the ghost boy showed up, I would've said that was the most ridiculous thing I'd ever heard. Now?

Hard pass on staring into the eyes, thanks.

Still, I'm not going to switch to a different person for my paper. Dad doesn't know it, but I chose Dexter for a reason. I wanted to write something *factual* about him, something that highlights the cool stuff he did while he was alive instead of the scary stories people tell about his grave now that he's dead. Dexter Graves may be just a ghost legend to a lot of people, but he was more than that in real life. He was a person. *Like the ghost boy.* As much as I want to hang out with Warner, I owe it to the ghost boy to figure out *his* story. Something is keeping him from resting in peace, and I don't care what it takes—I'm going to figure out what it is.

Warner nods. "I *might* have seen your proposal when you were turning it in to Ms. Medina. I figured if you thought he was a good person to write about, then he probably was."

He reaches back and rubs his neck awkwardly. He's nervous. My heart starts tap-dancing. Warner is nervous? About me, or about the history assignment? Could it possibly be both?

"I hope you aren't mad," Warner finishes. "It's just that you ace basically every test. And your dad *is* kind of an expert on that graveyard."

He's right. Dad is an expert on this subject. I just don't talk about that. I haven't since the day I caught Janice Reichert telling Annie Hayes that he holds séances in our kitchen. Plus, even though I hate to admit it, Sam is right about me being afraid. Graveyards scare me. Ghosts scare me. All that stuff scares me, and I'm done denying it.

The look on Warner's face tells me he's worried. I open my mouth to say it's okay, but he holds a hand up to stop me.

"Before you say anything, I *did* do some research on Dexter, so I know he was a dude who led some families here in the early 1800s. Like a settler or something." His eyes dart to mine nervously, then back down to the floor. "I'm not trying to cheat off you, I swear."

Little does Warner know that I couldn't be mad at him if I tried. Even if he lit my backpack on fire right now and then performed a never-rain-again dance, I'd still smile at him, because I can't help it. And cheat off me? Who is he kidding? I know for a fact that his grades are just as good as mine. I don't think he's trying to pair up with me because he needs to. I think it's because he *wants* to.

"I'm not mad."

Warner grins. His eyes twinkle.

"Working on it together sounds good. Sunday, maybe?" I ask. I'm shaking, I'm so nervous. I've never asked a boy to do anything with me before—not even study. "I'm around that day for sure."

And if this stupid ghost is still here by then, he's going to need to haunt someone else that afternoon.

Warner taps on his chin as if he's thinking. "Yeah, the project isn't due until next Friday, so I think that gives us enough time. Want to meet in the library? All you'll need to bring is your brain."

Now it's my turn to smile. All this time, I assumed Warner thought I was strange. I never once considered that I looked smart to him. Or anyone, for that matter.

"We don't need the library. Just meet me here in front of the school, and I'll take you where we need to go. By the time we're done, you'll know Dexter Graves like *he's* your cousin."

Warner shudders.

"What?" I ask.

"I saw a picture of his statue. I don't want to know him *that* well."

I laugh. "Fine. You'll know him well enough to get an A, then. How's that?"

"Perfect," he responds. "Oh, and Claire? Thanks."

Putting my lock back on, I smile at him. Not at the floor. Not at my shoes. At him. "No prob. See you then."

THIRTY-ONE

Sam, Casley, Emily, and I step off the bus at the intersection of Michigan and Wacker. It's freezing downtown, the air rushing off the lake carrying a bitter bite. I pull the hood of my coat up over my ears and tie it.

Sam laughs and jabs the pointy top of my hood. "You look exactly like a garden gnome."

I slap his hand away. I'll take looking like a garden gnome over having my ears freeze and fall off any day.

"Let's hurry. It's freezing. Plus, I don't want any of us getting home late," I say, rubbing the bracelet Emily gave me through my jacket sleeve as we get closer to the water. If there's ever a day I need bravery, it's today. Because this is going to suck.

The Clark Street Bridge is up right now. I stand at the base and stare up at it, a massive structure of metal beams rising into the pale blue sky. It's so strange how they can do that—take an entire street and crank it up into the air so boats can go through.

As we come up on the LaSalle Street Bridge, I notice that it has been raised, too. I also notice a large brown sign bolted to the ground at the foot of it. As we get closer, I gasp. There's an outline of the state of Illinois and the words THE EASTLAND DISASTER in bold letters on the top.

"I guess we found the spot," Emily says, snapping a picture of the sign with her phone. Her breath comes out in small white puffs. "So, this is where the boat sank?"

Looking down toward the water, I nod. There's a series of steps, about thirty of them, that lead down to the cement docking area. I walk down, the heels of my shoes tapping out a nervous rhythm. It seems so odd, this little river winding through the buildings towering over us. They look like stone giants, the sun glinting off their windows. But the river itself? I bet it looks exactly the same as it did that day in 1915. That horrible day.

"I did some reading on the *Eastland* last night," Emily says, her teeth chattering gently. "Did you guys know that the boat sank in only twenty feet of water? Twenty!"

Casley crouches down and stares at the river. "That's how shallow it is here?"

"Yup," I mumble. "Apparently, the boat was still docked when it started sinking. The orchestra on board kept playing, and they kept loading people on, even as it began to tip. By the time they realized something was wrong, most of the passengers had slid out into the water or were trapped beneath the boat."

Air hisses from between Sam's teeth. I can't tell if he's developing hypothermia or starting to freak out. Neither option is good.

I point a finger across the street at a huge reddish-brown building on the corner. "That's the Reid Murdoch Building. Apparently, they took most of the bodies there and put them in the basement for people to identify."

"It must have been so sad." Emily is looking out over the water, her cheeks flushed pink from the wind.

"If you guys don't mind, can I have a minute? I know it's cold and all, but I just need some time to sit here," I say, fixing my eyes on the dark water lapping against the cement dock in front of us.

My friends nod and take a seat on the steps.

There's the LaSalle Street Bridge on my left and the Clark Street Bridge on my right. Joggers trickle by. The air smells faintly like boat exhaust and fish, but every now and again I get a whiff of something darker. Something more frightening. It's a musty, watery smell that makes me feel anxious. Sirens echo off the buildings. I lean over the edge and look at my reflection in the water, shifting and shimmying in the sunlight. And then I startle so hard I nearly fall in.

He's here. The ghost boy. My reflection in the water is no longer my face but his. His dark eyes fix on mine, just like they did that night on the bus.

I scramble up and whirl around to find my friends. They're gone. Only the spot on the steps where they were just sitting isn't empty. My skin prickles with fear as I take in the scene unfolding around me: the bleakness of an overcast and muggy day; the drizzle falling from the gray sky; the crowd of people staring, wide-eyed and openmouthed, in my direction. And finally, the enormous boat overturned in the river. The SS *Eastland*.

Men are shouting, and bodies are flailing everywhere I look. The river is an actual sea of people—heads bobbing, arms thrashing, and sharp cries piercing my eardrums. The air is thick and warm and smells terrible. I cover my mouth, swallow the gag building my throat.

A few feet away, a man drags himself up onto the edge of the dock. The suit he's wearing is heavy and dripping with river water. He lies still for a moment, his forehead pressed against the rough cement. Then he coughs, and liquid spews from his mouth onto the ground. When he finally begins to breathe normally, he pulls himself upright, and before I can even ask him if he's okay, he plunges back into the dark water.

I'm paralyzed. Paralyzed with fear for myself. For the people bobbing in the water. For the nameless man who just jumped back in to save someone else, even though he barely survived the first time. I wonder who he went back for. A wife? A mother? A child? Part of me doesn't even want to know. I'm not sure I can handle it.

A loud squeaking sound draws my attention to a pulley lifting people from a hole in the side of the boat. Dozens of hands reach out to grab the wet woman twisting at the end of the rope and pull her to safety. She's alive. A man in some kind of old diving suit is perched on the edge of the half-submerged deck. His helmet is metal with tubes attached. He jumps into the water, and a large crowd cheers for him. They're on the Clark Street Bridge, so many people crammed almost on top of one another that I'm afraid it might collapse.

People are struggling at the surface of the water. I watch a few women be hoisted out. Their dresses are long and cumbersome, probably heavy enough to drag even the strongest woman straight to the bottom of the river if no hands reached out for her.

I am numb with shock. Numb with horror. Numb with the knowledge that this tragedy actually happened and the poor little ghost boy had to experience it. No wonder he's been haunting me. No one was fully prosecuted for the *Eastland* disaster, so his death is as unavenged as a death could possibly be.

Kneeling down at the edge of the water, I look for his face again. It's gone. My eyes linger there for a second before sliding up and focusing on the river as a whole. Everything is gone. The bobbing people. The overturned boat. The pulley and the diver. Even the Clark Street Bridge is empty and folded up toward the sky again. Blackness slowly creeps in, folding me up in its comfortable haze. I let go of everything—of the fear, the horror, the confusion rolling around inside me—and close my eyes. If it will make this vision go away, then the darkness can have me, for all I care.

THIRTY-TWO

I wake up and immediately shield my eyes. The sky is all I see, the sun beating down into my pupils so hard I feel like my head might split open. Something hard is beneath me. The voices of my friends are fuzzy and distant, like they are talking to me underwater.

Am I underwater? The thought terrifies me. I open my mouth, and a strange bleating sound comes out.

"I think we need to call nine-one-one." Casley's frantic voice carries on the wind. I try to say no, but my cardboard lips won't form the word.

Something shakes me, and my head lolls from side to side. "Hang on a sec, her eyes are open."

It's Sam. I can smell the candy on his breath. Even now, as I've got one foot in the grave, the kid is pigging out.

"I'm okay." My tongue finally cooperates. I hold a hand up to let them know I'm not dead. *Yet.*

"Gah. That was scary." A dark shadow passes over me. A shadow with coral lips. Emily. She crouches down so I can see her face clearly. It's worried. *Yikes.* I must have really put on a show just now.

Pulling myself up into a sitting position, I groan. Everything hurts. My entire body feels like someone took a meat tenderizer to it. I've seen Mom use one of those things, and they're scary.

"What happened?" I croak out.

"You were looking into the water, and then you just kinda spaced out for a minute. After that, you screamed and fell down," Casley says, her voice cracking nervously. "I wanted to call an ambulance, but Sam said you've passed out before."

Ugh. So glad my brother shared yet another thing about me that I'd rather keep to myself. I have passed out before. Many times, actually. Needles are my nemesis. All I have to do is think about them, and *bam*! Down I go. Only today was different. It wasn't a needle that sent me to the cold pavement. It was the ghost.

"Yeah, I've passed out before. It's all right. I'm feeling better." I rub my aching temples. Emily extends a hand. I grab it and pull myself to my feet. "I'm sorry I scared you guys."

"We're sorry you almost gave yourself a head injury," Casley says. "We tried to catch you, but you fell too fast."

"You sure you're okay?" Sam asks.

I nod. "Yup. Swear."

"Did you see something?" Emily asks.

I look back at the empty river. "I saw *everything*."

My legs are still shaking as I ease down onto the cold steps. My muscles are beginning to feel better, but my brain is still foggy. I remember a reflection in the water and the boat sleeping on its side. I remember the bodies and the chaos and the smell—like sour milk. I remember the long dresses and the man who dragged himself up on the dock. I remember the diver. I remember it all, and because of that, I feel terrible.

"He's definitely from the *Eastland*." I say this out loud because I know for a fact that it's true.

Sam sits down beside me. "Ghost boy? You saw him?"

"Sort of. I saw his reflection in the water, and then it was like I was there that day. The boat was tipped over right there." I point at the water just to our left. Thankfully, it isn't teeming with bodies anymore. "And there were people trying to swim. I think somehow he showed it to me. It was awful."

Emily drags a notebook from her bag. She flips to a page in the middle and taps a pencil on the paper. "Got it. So, did he ask that question again? 'Where are they?'"

"Nope. He didn't say anything." I sigh. "But seeing him again was helpful. I'm positive that if we find a picture of him online, I'll be able to recognize him now."

"Excellent," Emily says brightly. "Plus, you did what you came here for, right? You got the proof."

Detective Emily is right. I came here to test the hypothesis that the boy on the bus died in the *Eastland* disaster. After what he showed me just now, I have no doubt he did. I smile at her, feeling grateful. Casley was right; Emily is *great* at sleuthing, lip gloss and all.

"Yup. Now I just have to figure out exactly *who* he was," I answer, wringing my hands to bring some warmth back into the skin. "If I could find a passenger list, a list of everyone who was on the boat the day it sank, I could probably just use process of elimination to narrow down the possibilities. There couldn't have been *that* many boys his age on the boat."

Sam casts a doubtful look in my direction. "Uh, I don't know about that. There could've been. Didn't you say there were a lot of entire families that boarded the boat that day?"

"Yeah, but that's where pictures will come in," Emily says, tapping her pencil against her notebook. "Claire knows what the boy looks like now. If we can find a list with *pictures* of the passengers, she'll be able to match up the boy's face to his name."

I sigh, concern churning in me. Dad once told me that a long time ago, people didn't get pictures taken unless they were important or rich. If the boy on the bus was neither, we've gotta hope he had at least one picture taken in his short life. My eyes glide back to the Reid Murdoch Building. I imagine people hauling body after body into that basement, then waiting for friends and relatives to show up and give them names. Without the internet and cell phones, that must have taken forever! I wonder how they kept them all organized without knowing who they were...

Organized. My brain snags on the thought. The scuba divers and nurses and police officers couldn't identify everyone they pulled out of the water, right? It wouldn't have been possible when there were so many people on the boat. They probably had a system—a method of labeling to keep all those poor people straight until their families could get there and identify them. I shrug the backpack from my shoulders and slide the paper I found on the bus from the middle of my science textbook.

"What if this wasn't a receipt or a dry-cleaning tag?" I ask, waving it in the air.

"What else could it be?" Casley asks tentatively.

"A label." Tugging my cell phone from my pocket, I pull up Google. "Think like a scientist for a minute, guys. If you were conducting an experiment that involved taking hundreds of different samples from, say, a lake or something, you wouldn't just throw them all into one container and get them all mixed up, right?"

Understanding dawns on Casley. "Ohhhh! You'd label them. Specimen A, specimen B, et cetera."

"Right! That's what we did for our science experiment last year, the one on algae blooms, remember? We had a test sample, and then every other sample we experimented with was labeled with a letter."

Sam chuckles. "Wow."

"Impressed?" Casley asks, lifting an eyebrow.

"With how dorky you guys are? Totally!"

She leans over to punch him, but Emily beats her to it. "You're just jealous they're figuring this out instead of you, tough guy."

"Riiiiight," Sam mocks, grinning widely. "That's it."

That *is* it, but I don't say that. Sam claims he knows me better than anyone, and that's true, but so is the opposite. I know him better than anyone, too. I know he only smiles like this at people he truly likes.

I am *so* going to tease him about this later.

"Okay, okay. Back to the ghost. I think I know how to figure out who he was." My thumb hovers over the screen of my phone. Once I press this button, there's no going back. Either I'll discover the identity of the little boy I've been seeing for a week and the mystery will be solved, or I'll be just as lost as I was last night when Sam and I decided to come here looking for answers.

Sam peers over my shoulder, then reads aloud the words I typed into the search bar: "who is little boy 396." His eyes meet mine. "We've searched basically everything *but* that. You think this will do it?"

"Only one way to find out." I push enter before I can chicken out. I read the headline. Once. Twice. Three times. My heart nearly stops beating.

WHOSE IS THIS LITTLE BOY? NO. 396 AT THE MORGUE

It's a copy of a *Chicago Tribune* article from July 27, 1915. I let my eyes wander down to the text below the headline and begin reading out loud:

"Whose little boy is that?"
Almost every one seeking relatives or friends at the Second Regiment armory morgue has asked the question as they passed the body of a dark, curly

haired boy, between 8 and 9 years old. Some mothers, looking for their own babies, have shed their tears over him as they gazed at the little face. Sadly they have shaken their heads and asked the question. The body, numbered 396, has been there since 4 o'clock Saturday afternoon. The boy had been dressed all in white.

A hushed silence falls over the group. Nothing but the sound of water gently lapping breaks the quiet for a long moment.

Sam takes the phone from my hands and pulls up a different article. "This says that after the boat sank, the victims were laid out in the basement so people could identify them, just like you said. *But*, according to this, all of the bodies were identified several days after the boat tipped. All of them *except* one."

He hands me back the phone. A grainy, black-and-white image sits just below the article. It's a little boy in a hat. Big, piercing eyes stare into the camera—the same eyes I just saw in the water. The same eyes that have been haunting me for days. It's him. It's my ghost boy.

"Willie Novotny, age seven," I whisper. It's the first time I've said his name out loud, and the sound turns my skin into gooseflesh.

"Yup. This says they had no idea what his name was, so he was labeled 'Boy 396.'" He pulls his hood up over his head, blocking the wind. "Boy 396 was there for an entire week."

I open my hand and let go of the paper I found on the bus. It flutters down to the water, landing faceup in the dark, lapping waves. Normally, I'd scramble onto my hands and knees to pull it out so I'm not littering, but not today. Today I'm letting it go. I watch the hastily scribbled numbers sink below the surface, my stomach twisting into a painful knot. I can't look at the picture anymore. I close the article and shove my phone back into my pocket. Then I look back toward the water. It's calmer now, almost peaceful as it ripples past us. But I know the truth. It isn't calm. It isn't peaceful. It's the water that sucked that poor little boy down, then left him alone in a cold stone basement. How could such a thing happen in water only twenty feet deep and with land so close? Like the Iroquois Theater fire, it seems so...unbelievable.

Casley steps forward. The excitement of our break-through has drained from her eyes, and she looks fearful. "Are you *sure* he's the one haunting you? All the evidence seems to fit, but I know you. You're...*skeptical.*"

Not anymore, I'm not. The lump in my throat grows bigger. "I'm positive. It makes sense. Willie was left alone. For days. He has a lot of reasons to be unhappy."

Sam nods somberly. "Apparently, his parents were killed on the boat, so there was no one to identify him. Not right away, at least."

"So, the question he was asking makes sense now," Emily says.

"What?" I'm so lost in the rippling of the river that I barely hear her.

Emily taps her notepad, her index finger pausing over the page she has open. "*Where are they.* I've been thinking about that ever since you mentioned it when we were researching in your living room. It makes sense now. Maybe the ghost was looking for his parents."

Oh my god. I think about the first time I saw the ghost boy, Willie, mouthing this to me, when the *feeling* started up. I thought *I* was missing something or that something of mine was lost. Never once did I consider that it was the ghost boy who was missing something. His family. He was missing his family.

Guess the broken family picture was a good clue after all.

THIRTY-THREE

The echoes of the past grow quieter with each step I take away from the river. I don't know how I'll ever figure out what Willie Novotny wants from me, or why he started haunting me to begin with, but I have to. Flooded houses and temporary lockers demand it.

"Are you okay?" Sam asks as he climbs onto the bus. We walked to Michigan Avenue to catch the 146 bus since it should get us home the fastest. "You're so quiet."

"I'm okay. Just worried."

Sitting down, he pats the seat next to him. "About what? You know who the ghost is now."

"Yeah, but that doesn't solve everything. It only solves one part of the puzzle." I try not to sound frustrated, but it's hard. No matter how I look at this situation, it's still stinky. "So,

Willie Novotny is the ghost haunting me. The big question is why."

Sam appears to be lost in thought for a minute. He's staring out the window at the blur of trees and lake rushing by. I look out just as Navy Pier whooshes past. The huge Ferris wheel looks cool set against the bright blue sky, and all of the cruise boats are gleaming in the sun. Chicago really is beautiful. Even if there is a ghost in it that's determined to keep me awake every night.

"Maybe the *why* doesn't matter anymore," Sam finally says with a shrug. "He might have just wanted someone to find him, you know? Someone who cares about his story, not just the stuff Dad talks about on his ghost tours."

I nod along with this. Sam could be right. After all, that's why I chose Dexter Graves for my history project. Still, the feeling isn't gone. "It's not over. I can still feel him, Sam. If the ghost boy were satisfied, wouldn't he be gone by now?"

Sam scratches his head. "I just don't get it. I read that when Willie's body was finally identified, there was a huge parade for him, and thousands of people showed up. People who didn't even know him. He became, like, this symbol— like, he represented all the people who died, not just himself. I don't know what you could possibly do for him that an entire parade didn't do."

"Not sure, but I do have an idea," I whisper. "Last night, before I fell asleep, I remembered reading that there are a few places in Chicago that have information or exhibits on the SS *Eastland*. The biggest one is the Chicago History Museum."

"You think there might be information on Willie there?" Sam asks hopefully.

"Maybe," I respond. "It's worth a try."

I flip my backpack around and tug the zipper open. Fishing through broken pencils, folders, and erasers, I finally dig out a crumpled ten-dollar bill. "I wonder what it costs to get in. I only have ten bucks and a Dunkin' Donuts gift card."

Sam sighs. "Ugh. I don't know. Lemme see what I have."

While he's rifling through his backpack, I pull up the museum website and click on the admission page. "Oh my gosh! Sam! It's free if you're twelve or under!"

My brother smiles the smile of a person who's just won something. "Awesome. You can get in free, and I'm sure the ten bucks will cover my ticket. Now we just need to convince them to let us in."

I hadn't thought of that. Two kids, no adults? There's no way we're going to get in there today.

"What are you two whispering about?" Emily is beside us, her body swaying back and forth with the motion of the bus. She's holding on to those little handle thingies that come down from the top of the roof. Rookie error. Always hold on to the pole—it's sturdier.

"We're going to the museum to do a little more research," Sam answers.

Emily's eyebrows knit together. "Ugh. Wish I could go, too."

"No worries. We'll text you guys if we find out anything good." I drop my phone back into my bag and zip it back up. Then I peek up at the CTA map posted on the side of the bus. Blue, red, green, and purple lines snake across the white paper, showing different stops all across the city. I squint at it, trying to figure out where we are in that mess. "How are we going to get there?"

"Uber," Sam says with a smirk.

"Really? You know how to call one?"

"Yup. I put the app on my phone a month ago and convinced Dad to let me enter his credit card information." He swipes a finger across his home screen, and the Uber app appears.

"How does it work, exactly? Do we need more than ten bucks?" I ask, feeling hopeful. Maybe this little research trip is going to work out okay after all.

He clicks on the icon and brings up a map. There are

little dots pulsing all over it. "As soon as we get off this bus, I'll call one. It will come pick us up, and the charge will go straight to Dad's credit card."

This makes my ears perk up. "Straight to Dad's card? So, will he know where we went?"

"I don't know," he admits. "He'll see the amount and probably the day, but I don't know if he can see where we went."

Nope. No way. "Too risky. We're grounded, remember?" I say. "If Mom and Dad find out we aren't working on something for school, they're going to be so mad."

"We can't get in any more trouble than we're already in, Claire!" Sam exclaims. "Plus, this is research. It's almost like homework. We'll look at a few other exhibits there, too. It will be like a school field trip."

Right. A school field trip. Only instead of looking at dinosaur bones or mummies or butterfly havens, we're looking for ghost clues. Jeez. Sometimes I think my life would make a perfect episode of *Scooby-Doo*.

I glance back toward the end of the bus where Emily has sat back down with Casley. They give a little wave, and I wave back. I know they need to go home, but I wish they were coming with us. I stifle a laugh, thinking that in a twisted way, it's Willie's doing. He brought us together. Even if this ghost never goes away, even if the séance rumors start back up again and I can never walk through the alley without counting, I finally have a circle of friends, and they're the best.

"Claire?" Sam says, snapping his fingers in front of my face.

"Yeah?"

"What other choice do we have?"

None. Absolutely none.

I smile weakly. For once, my brother is 100 percent correct. "Okay, let's do it. But we need to move fast."

THIRTY-FOUR

The Chicago History Museum is pretty. I think most museums are pretty, actually, but this one is especially so. We've just walked through the front doors and past a weird old car that is on display in the lobby. It looks like something my dad would think is cool.

By the time we get our tickets, my heart is racing. "Do you know where the exhibit is?" I ask Sam.

He shrugs. "Never been here before."

I laugh. "Yes, you have. All the fifth-grade classes come here for a field trip."

Sam groans. "Fine. I've been here. I just didn't pay attention, okay?"

I roll my eyes. He better pay attention now. Our lives depend on it. I turn back toward the man who sold us our tickets. "Excuse me, do you know where the *Eastland* exhibit is?"

Just as he's about to answer, a woman steps out from behind the counter, smiling warmly. "It's on the second floor, but if you'd like to follow me, I'll walk you there."

We follow our guide up a flight of stairs and through several winding hallways covered in black-and-white photos of Chicago history. In the center of the wing we enter next, there's an entire El car positioned front and center. It's old, maybe from the early 1900s, and gorgeous. Never thought I'd say that about an El car, but this one is unique. It's wooden and has bright stained glass windows. I think back on the last time I took the El with Dad. It was crowded, dirty, and smelled a little like cat pee. Apparently, taking public transportation was way more luxurious back in the day.

I poke Sam in the ribs as we pass an exhibit about the Great Chicago Fire. It's huge. It's also very busy. There are pictures, quotes, and maps plastered all over the walls from the floor up. There's even a replica of the water tower and a porcelain doll that survived the fire! About a dozen people mill around the display, taking it all in. I think about the fires that swept across the city—across Lincoln Park—and destroyed everything, including the gravestones from the city cemetery. Hard to imagine that only three hundred people died in a fire that lasted two full days, but more than double that number died on the *Eastland*, which sank in less than five minutes.

Across from that is a display on the Haymarket Riot. It's colorful and vibrant. A group of children in the same color T-shirt are looking at it while a woman explains the event. Must be some kind of after-school club.

"Here we are. You did say the *Eastland* disaster, correct?" the woman asks.

I nod and follow her to a small area where I expect to find a small crowd like there was over by the Great Chicago Fire exhibit. The museum is jammed today, and no doubt a disaster as epic as the *Eastland* has drawn a lot of interest.

Instead, the first thing I see is a wheel. It's one of those big wooden ones with handles jutting out. The kind of wheel that was used to steer boats a long time ago. That's cool—I had assumed everything from the *Eastland* was destroyed when it sank. There's also a large metal pipe in a display attached to the wall. The card beneath it tells me it was the iron whistle from the *Eastland*. *Wow.* I imagine the man responsible for blowing it on the day of the disaster, how hard he must have tried to warn everyone.

When I finally tear my eyes away from the whistle, I do a quick glance around the area, and my mouth flops open. There's *no one* here. No wall of bodies. No students on a field trip. No people doing research. No tourists chattering away. Not even one single person is looking at the *Eastland* exhibit.

"The *Eastland* is one of our city's least-talked-about disasters," our chaperone states. "I'm impressed your teacher chose it to discuss. What class is your project for?"

"It's...ah...an independent study kind of class," I answer numbly as I stare at the empty space. How is this section so empty when the others are so crowded that you can barely walk?

Sam draws closer to the display. His eyes are fixed on a wooden chair inside a glass case. Stamped into the wood on the back is the word EASTLAND in caps. "Whoa. This is amazing."

"I know," I reply. I've found a picture of an older man in suspenders holding a waterlogged child in his arms. The child looks lifeless. Dead. Looking away, I tell myself to stop being a chicken. This is history. It's important. It's also painful, but looking at pictures like this one is the only way to show respect. To remember what happened.

And that is *exactly* what no one else seems to be doing. In fact, it seems like the entire city has forgotten the *Eastland*. I look back at the black-and-white image of the man holding the child. His eyes are big and bugged out like he'd just seen the worst thing imaginable. I think he had.

"You know, the *Eastland* disaster killed more passengers

than the *Titanic*," our guide says. I think she's trying to keep us talking. "Have you heard of the *Titanic*?"

"Who hasn't heard of the *Titanic*?" Sam asks with a snort.

"Right, well, it's definitely one of the more popular disasters. Television and movies have done a lot to increase awareness of it. Very little has been done on the *Eastland*, and as a result, many people have never heard of it. Not even folks who live in Chicago."

My heart hurts. After seeing that day in the vision Willie gave me, I can't imagine how such a tragic event has been forgotten. The fear and the pain on the faces of the people are things I'll remember for the rest of my life.

"I'm confused, though," Sam says. "Didn't like, a thousand people die on the *Titanic*? That's way more than the *Eastland*."

"True," she responds. "The exact number of people who died on the *Titanic* varies depending on who you ask, but most sources say it was around fifteen hundred. That's definitely more total deaths than on the SS *Eastland*."

Sam goes to question her again, but she holds a finger up. "All fifteen hundred of those people weren't passengers, though. Many were crew. Around eight hundred and thirty-two were actually passengers, whereas on the *Eastland*, there were eight hundred and forty-one *passengers* who died."

"Wow," Sam breathes out. "Why did it sink, anyway?"

"Unfortunately, there were several reasons. For one, a lot of life jackets and safety boats were added to the *Eastland* shortly before this journey. That added a great deal of weight to a boat that was already known to be somewhat unstable. To make matters worse, all of that extra weight was added to the upper deck."

"The top of the boat?" I ask incredulously. I did an extra-credit science experiment once on the center of gravity. You can balance a wooden ruler on your finger at exactly the six-inch mark. That's where its center of gravity is—the point where the gravitational pull on both sides is even. Adding anything heavy to the top of a boat would change its center of gravity and make it easier for the boat to tip, right? "Wouldn't the top be the worst place for them to put the extra boats and life jackets?"

"Unfortunately, yes." She nods. "The extra supplies made it top-heavy. Plus, there were too many people on board, and the boat simply wasn't designed well."

Too many people on board. People who were thrilled to be going on a boat like this, some of them for the first time in their lives. I can imagine how they filed onto the deck with excitement, their long dresses and stifling suits making the summer day feel stickier than usual. Little did any of them know that it was the last time they'd ever wear those fancy clothes. My mind swims with dark thoughts, and then, like a pawn in the game of Sorry!, it lands back on Willie.

No wonder Willie doesn't trust my parents. He probably doesn't trust *any* adults. They took him on a boat, promised him an amazing day, but instead, he drowned. *He trusts me*, I remind myself. *He trusts me to fix this for him, and that's exactly what I'm going to do.*

"What about Willie?" I ask. There are framed pictures of the boat and the lines outside of the Reid Murdoch Building. There's also a picture of the diver in the metal helmet I saw in the vision and the actual iron whistle from the boat. There are maps and letters and documents galore. But there's no Willie. "Do you have anything on Willie Novotny?"

"Novotny, Novotny," our guide repeats. "No, that name doesn't ring a bell. I'm so sorry. Was he a survivor?"

"No. He was a little boy whose family died on the boat that day. He died as well, but he was left behind in the morgue, because no one was left to identify him."

Her face lights up with recognition. "Oh, yes. The cabinetmaker's son, right?"

I shrug. I have no idea if Willie Novotny's father was a cabinetmaker.

She scribbles something down on her clipboard. "Twenty-two entire families perished on the *Eastland*, and if

I'm right about who you are talking about, then no, we have nothing on him here in the display. We might in the research center, though. Perhaps you could find something in the archives on him. I'm sorry."

Warning bells go off in my brain. This museum has the largest collection of *Eastland* disaster information anywhere in the city, yet there's *no one* looking at it. There's also nothing on Willie Novotny, or Boy 396, anywhere. Missing. Something is missing. No, *everything* is missing.

"Thank you, we appreciate this." I say, tugging Sam in the direction of the exit. Suddenly, it all makes sense to me. Willie Novotny was forgotten in the morgue after that horrible tragedy, and he's still being forgotten now.

"Is that all you need? I'm more than happy to show you more..." our guide says as we hurry away from her.

But she can't show us more, right? It's awesome that they have an exhibit dedicated to the *Eastland*, but their little corner of history with no visitors and no Willie is all they have. And it's not enough. Not nearly enough.

I'm so sorry, Willie.

THIRTY-FIVE

The house smells like cinnamon when Sam and I get home. I've always thought cinnamon is the friendliest of Mom's baking smells. It's spicy and sweet and makes the house feel like one big hug. But today, it doesn't give me the warm fuzzies at all. Today, it just makes me wonder if Willie Novotny liked cinnamon in his applesauce, or if he ever had a cookie with cinnamon baked into it. I hope so.

"I can't believe no one was even looking at the exhibit," Sam says glumly, as if reading my thoughts. "I bet if we asked one hundred kids in our school about the *Eastland*, we would get one hundred confused looks."

Sinking down onto the couch, I sigh. "It all makes sense to me now."

"What? The haunting stuff?"

"Yeah. Think about it. Willie died, and no one was ever fully prosecuted for the boat sinking, right? Also, he was left in the morgue *alone* for a week." Just the idea creeps me out. I have never seen a morgue, but I know they're scary. "He's got a lot of reasons to haunt someone."

Sam fidgets with the ties on his hoodie. His eyes are crinkled up in either worry or confusion. "But why you?"

This is where my mind draws a blank. We may have figured out that Willie doesn't trust adults, but that still doesn't explain why he chose me. There are so many kids in Chicago. Surely there's at least one who would've been a better fit? Maybe one who did a research paper on the *Eastland*, or one who's more like my dad and loves ghost legends. Why wouldn't Willie have chosen someone like that to haunt?

Unless...

Unless Willie wasn't just looking for someone who knew the facts. Maybe he was looking for someone who understood how he felt. Someone who felt like everyone was moving on without them.

Like me.

I sit completely still for a moment, the hairs on my arms and the back of my neck slowly rising like zombies from the dead. Up until this week, I thought Casley was trying to leave me behind! I misunderstood everything she did. I even misunderstood Emily. Willie Novotny thinks everyone forgot about him, and his restless spirit has been looking for someone to help him fix it all these years.

Look for the story history doesn't tell, because that might be the one that matters. My mom's words echo through my head. Whoa. That wasn't just *a* teachable moment—it was *the* teachable moment, the message Willie wanted me to get all this time!

I fly up off the couch and sprint to the kitchen. Mom is standing at the oven, both hands covered in fluffy mitts and a trademark splash of white powder dusted across her nose. Without warning, I throw my arms around her and breathe out a thank-you.

"Good heavens!" Mom laughs, stumbling under the weight of my hug. "You're welcome. But...for what?"

"Has anyone ever told you that you'd make a great teacher?"

Mom's flour-covered face lights up. I may regret saying that, but I had to. Mom's teachable moments aren't just an annoying habit. They're important. *Really* important.

I'm going to listen to them from now on.

THIRTY-SIX

Experiment, analyze the data, and draw a conclusion. Those are the final steps of the scientific method—the ones that can either make or break a scientist. Right now, my hopes are soaring, because I finally know why Willie picked me! I also know what he wants, and I'm positive I can give it to him.

I throw my father's office door open. He's sitting at the desk, hunched over his laptop. Dad's eyes widen for a moment, and then he puts a hand on his chest and laughs. "Claire! Good grief, you scared me! What's up?"

"Boy three hundred and ninety-six!" I blurt out, grimacing as my brother skids into the room and slams into my back.

Dad tilts his head to the side. "What?"

"You said your publisher wants you to write another book, right?"

"Yes," Dad says calmly. "They want a second book. What about it?"

"You have to include the SS *Eastland* disaster. And Willie Novotny. He was seven years old, and his father was a Czech cabinetmaker."

"Czech?" Sam pipes up behind me. Guess I forgot to tell him I did a little digging on the way home from the museum. He's not the only one who knows how to use Google.

"Yes, they were immigrants from Austria-Hungary, which is now the Czech Republic," I tell him breathlessly.

Dad still looks confused, so I continue. "Willie died on the SS *Eastland*, but no one identified his body for a week because his family was killed, too."

My father is quiet. Too quiet. I wring my hands nervously, wishing I could read his mind.

"Remember how Mom said you tell the stories that get forgotten? Well, the *Eastland* has been forgotten. And Willie has, too. His story is important, and it's not fair that no one knows it."

I'm rattling on, but I don't care. I have to tell him this stuff. He's the only person who can fix this for Willie now—I'm sure of it.

Dad slips the reading glasses from his face. He sets them on the table slowly, carefully. I'm worried he doesn't understand what I'm saying, mostly because I know how strange all of this must sound. But also because this book is bigger than me. It's bigger than Dad. It's the story of a disaster that took over eight hundred lives that day in 1915.

The man with suspenders holding the wet boy in his arms.

The diver who spent days plunging into that cold, black water to pull people out.

The people who watched from the Clark Street Bridge.

The Red Cross volunteers who looked after Willie's body day after day, waiting for someone to show up and claim him.

The city of Chicago was changed by the SS *Eastland* sinking, yet no one remembers.

But they will...

Dad's book sold to a huge publisher, and maybe he can't even decide what's going to be in it without getting permission. But I know one thing for sure: Willie deserves more than an empty exhibit at the local museum and a few measly articles online. And I won't stop until I make him happy...until I find a way to keep his memory alive.

"A Czech cabinetmaker, huh?" Dad asks quietly. It snaps me from my thoughts.

"Yes," I whisper. "His family was one of twenty-two entire families that died that day."

"How do you know all of this?" Dad asks, raising a scrutinizing eyebrow.

Because Willie has been haunting me.

I shrug, unsure of exactly how to answer. "I'm a scientist. Research is my jam."

"Well, I guess it's my *jam*, too." Dad smiles, then turns his laptop to face me. My breath catches. His screen is filled with a picture of Willie.

"You...you already knew who Willie was?" I stammer.

"Yes. I've known about Willie and his family for a while now. The night you helped me on the ghost tour, I decided that if I had an opportunity to write a second book, I'd feature the *Eastland*. I was considering focusing on one family who boarded the boat that day. I just hadn't decided on which family. *Until now*," he says.

I swallow hard. "So, you'll do it? You'll write a chapter about Willie?"

"I'll do more than write one chapter. I'll write several. On one condition, though," he answers.

"What?" Sam and I ask in unison.

Whatever it is, you got this. I repeat this over and over in my head as I wait for Dad's response. There's nothing I can't handle. Willie deserves it. The passengers who died deserve it.

"The condition is that you'll help me. You know, be a research assistant of sorts."

I must've misunderstood him. "Research assistant?"

Dad stands from his computer and walks over to the small set of bookshelves in his office. "Yes! Like you said, you're a scientist. You do impeccable research. Plus, it took a lot of guts to help me on that tour, Claire. I know you didn't like it much. I also know something spooked you that night."

I do a double take. "Wait. What? How did you know?"

"Hmm, let me think." He lifts a hand to his chin dramatically, a teasing smile perched on his face. "Maybe it was the fact that you fell off your seat looking for a boy who was never on the bus, or that you barely said three words on our way home that night. Or that when I came home from work the next day, you were shaking like a leaf and talking about storms that hadn't happened. Or—"

I wave a hand in the air to stop him. "If you knew all that, why didn't you say anything?"

His eyes soften. "I didn't realize it was all connected. Not at first, anyway. It wasn't until I started thinking about the flooding story you and Sam told that I started putting the pieces together."

"So, we aren't grounded anymore?"

"You aren't grounded anymore," he confirms. Still, his tone is somber. "Your mother and I talked about it earlier today and decided we aren't going to push you to explain. We trust you'll come to us when you're ready to talk about it."

Just like Sam finally went to them about his math test when he was ready. Only I never went to Dad. I was so afraid that he'd become even more obsessed with ghosts that I didn't give him a chance.

"I'm sorry I didn't tell you. I guess I wanted to handle it on my own."

"I should be the one apologizing, honey. I think you wanted to handle it on your own because you were scared and didn't trust me not to make it worse." There's pain in his voice. A raw sadness I've never heard from him, even when he and Mom worry about money. "I hope you and your brother know that nothing is more important to me than you. Not books. Not tour buses. *Nothing.*"

"I know," I whisper. Sam was right. Dad doesn't care more about his ghosts than us. He's just following his dreams. Doing what he loves, like Mom with JuliCakes. Like Sam with hockey. Me with science. Even though I'll never love the Spirits bus, I get it now. Telling these stories is important to Dad. Without them, the truth gets forgotten.

"Is everything all right now?" Dad's voice is tight. Concerned.

I look at Sam and smile. "Yeah. It is."

I almost tell him about seeing Willie for the first time, but something stops me. This time it isn't because I don't trust him. It's because out of everyone on the tour bus that night, Willie came to *me*. Only me.

"Look," Dad starts. "I have a lot of research on the *Eastland* built up and even more books that cover the disaster in detail. And you—you've clearly gathered a lot as well. Between the two of us, we should be able to piece together a clear picture of what happened that day and retell it from the Novotny family's point of view."

I try to ease down into his corner chair, but instead I stumble over a stack of paper and fall.

Sam laughs. He lifts a hand to his mouth as if he's holding a microphone. "Claire Koster, everybody. Good research skills, bad coordination."

"Shut up," I say, lobbing a throw pillow at his head. He ducks it and wags a finger in the air.

"Your name will be in the acknowledgments," Dad says. "I'll make sure of it. And we can use whatever research methods you prefer. The reigning champion of the science fair clearly knows how to research thoroughly."

I take a second to savor the moment. Somehow, I've gone from hating everything about Dad's books and tour bus to working with him.

"So, can I presume you are in?" Dad asks.

I couldn't be more in if I tried. "Yes. Yes!"

Dad grins. It's almost as big as the day he told me about the book deal. I smile back, because this is the best day of my life. I've been scared of all this ghost stuff for as long as I can remember, but admitting it made me feel weak. Ashamed. Not anymore. Everyone has problems: divorces, sick parents, bills, failing math scores. What matters is how you handle them. Thanks to Willie, I'm done hiding mine.

No. More. Secrets.

THIRTY-SEVEN

"396" THIS LITTLE *EASTLAND* VICTIM IS
IDENTIFIED AT LAST. Two boys yesterday
identified body no. 396 as Willie Novotny, their
seven-year-old playmate.

—*Chicago Tribune*, Friday, July 30, 1915

The entrance to Bohemian National Cemetery doesn't look
like I expected it to. Instead, it looks like a fortress or a castle,
something medieval. Sam and I walk through together, but
once we get inside the gate, he stops.

"You okay?" I ask, slowing down.

Rubbing the back of his neck, he nods. "Yeah. Just feeling
a little nervous. Aren't you?"

Truth is, I thought I'd be nervous. I thought I'd be so scared to look for Willie's grave that I'd throw up in the Uber on the way here, or worse, chicken out. But now that we're here, I feel different. Better.

I lift my chin and smile into the sun, savoring the heat on my cheeks. For the first time in weeks, it looks and feels like spring. Vibrant green buds fill out the trees. The tips of delicate flowers are beginning to break through the soil. The chill in the air is almost completely gone, replaced with a soft warmth that reminds me of Mom's fresh-baked cookies.

"I feel good about this. We've already solved the mystery *and* hopefully given Willie what he wanted."

"Then why are we here?" my brother asks warily.

"To say goodbye."

It has been one week since Willie first appeared on the tour bus. The exact same amount of time Willie was waiting in the basement of the Reid Murdoch Building for someone to come claim him. Maybe that's just a coincidence, but I don't think so. I think Willie is expecting us to come here today.

The breeze picks up, sprinkling the sidewalk with freshly cut grass like a living welcome mat. Maybe it's Willie's way of beckoning us in, telling us that we shouldn't be afraid. I take out the map I printed from the Bohemian Cemetery website and flatten it against the wall.

"According to this, the people who died on the *Eastland* are buried in section sixteen." I glance up and point to our left. "It should be directly that way."

Sam looks out over the headstones, then arches an eyebrow as he dramatically sweeps a hand out over the pavement. "Since you're feeling so good about this...after you."

I brush past him, determined not to show fear. Ghosts may not be as simple to understand as litmus paper, but that doesn't mean they're bad. Willie's not. He just needed help. Like Emily! Good thing they weren't as stubborn as I was about asking for it. I waited way too long to tell Casley about my problem and ended up crying on a nasty bathroom floor because of it. Even if they're embarrassing or scary, I'll never keep secrets like that again.

The sidewalk winds through clusters of headstones, statues, and trees. Birds call out to one another, and clouds lazily roll past. Things feel so different than they did back when Willie first made contact that it's hard to believe this is the same Chicago. Part of me says it's just how seasons work. It is spring, after all. Another part of me says it's more than that. It's a new beginning for Willie. And me.

"Claire," Sam hisses. "Look."

My thoughts scatter as I follow the tip of Sam's finger to the flash of green up ahead. It's a ship steering wheel, half-buried in a large cement block. A new chill rushes up my spine, only this time it feels like excitement rather than fear.

We're close.

A few strides later, we're standing in front of the wheel. The letters etched into the front of the cement block say SS EASTLAND, and the red bricks surrounding it have names on them. Vibrant purple flowers ring the edges of the bricks. It's beautiful.

"It must be some kind of memorial or something. To the people who died on the boat, I guess," I say, gently trailing a finger along the wheel's handles.

Scanning the headstones in the area, I pause when one catches my eye. It's dark gray—almost black—and the last name stands out. Novotny. Taking care not to stomp on any flowers, I make my way to the stone.

"Rodina Novotny," I breathe out. "Weird. I don't remember reading anything about someone in Willie's family named Rodina."

Sam shakes his head. "Me neither. His mother's name was Agnes. Maybe it was a grandmother?"

I turn in a full circle, confused. There's only one grave marked Novotny, and we don't even recognize the first name on it. There isn't a grave for Willie's parents, sister, or him. It makes no sense, not that anything that has to do with ghosts ever really does.

An idea pops into my head. "Sam, can I see your phone?"

He looks at me quizzically. "Yeah. Why?"

"I'm going to look up the word *rodina*. Maybe it isn't a name."

Sam shrugs. "Okay, but it's capitalized like a name."

I type in "what does the word *rodina* mean" and with a few swipes, suck in a sharp breath. Angling the phone screen toward Sam, I share what I've discovered. "Family. This says *Rodina* means family in Czech."

The Novotny family. One headstone, four people. I squat down and run a hand over the grass beneath my feet. This is it, Willie's final resting place.

I'm about to use Sam's phone to snap a picture of the grave so I don't have to dig mine out of my bag when something stops me. The chill of invisible fingers on mine. They slide into my hand and squeeze, taking my breath away. For a split second, everything stops. The birds go silent, the clouds hang frozen in the blue sky, and a feeling of contentment trickles into my body. Willie is here, except unlike the time he found me in the bathroom at school, he's not upset.

My stillness tips Sam off to Willie's presence. Shadows of concern linger on his face as he studies me. "Is it still there? The feeling of something missing?"

The fingers clenching my hand give one final squeeze,

then drift away on a flower-scented breeze. I swallow back tears of joy and shake my head. "No. He's happy."

"And you? Are you happy?" Sam asks, hope lacing his words.

I don't even need to think about his question. We did the impossible. We solved the mystery I thought was unsolvable, and we made a one-hundred-plus-year-old ghost happy at the same time. I'm not just happy; I'm thrilled.

Reaching up to sling my arm around my brother, I smile. "Couldn't be happier, dork. Let's go home."

EPILOGUE

"A ninety-four? How did you pull that off?" Casley exclaims as we cross through the thick black gates of Graceland Cemetery.

Sam winks in my direction. "Eh, math isn't so bad. I just wasn't studying right."

I grin. I've been helping Sam study for more than a month now, and he hasn't needed to hide failed tests in those ugly dumpsters even once. In fact, he hasn't gotten lower than an eighty-two since the test he failed! It was the least I could do, since he helped me so much with the ghost and all. As long as I never have to go back to sleeping in my closet, Sam will be one of the top-scoring students in pre-algebra. I'll make sure of it.

And as for Willie—well, he hasn't haunted me since the day I said goodbye to him at the cemetery. No fluttering curtains, no numbers streaked across the shower wall, no bad feelings or ghostly whispers. I can't say I miss him, because the whole ghost thing was a lot to handle, but I miss the mystery.

My promise to Willie didn't stop after I agreed to help Dad, though. After my parents bought me a membership to the Chicago History Museum so I could use their research room, I started going there every weekend. I told the people who work there about Dad's new book and my research on the *Eastland* disaster. I also told them about Willie and how important he was. The manager was so impressed that she asked me to be a part-time volunteer every Saturday morning! Sometimes it's little kids I'm working with, and sometimes it's adults. But the *who* doesn't really matter all that much. What matters is that I have the chance to talk about the SS *Eastland* and Willie. I always make sure to show his picture, too. If I have anything to say about it, he'll never be forgotten again.

Turning to look at the person on my right, I feel my smile widen. Warner is keeping pace with us, his eyes twinkling in the muted late-afternoon sunlight. He slows to a stop just inside the entrance of the graveyard.

"Whoa," he whispers.

Whoa is right. Graceland is huge and beautiful. Hauntingly beautiful. Giant trees dripping down over the bony-white headstones, chipped mausoleums standing like rows of soldiers, and elegant sculpted figures spiraling into the sky... It's enough to make you almost forget about the death.

Almost.

"You good?" I ask Warner.

"Yeah." He sweeps his arms out over the spread of gravestones surrounding us. "Considering where we are, I'm surprisingly good."

"Anyone else have that déjà vu feeling?" Casley asks as she unzips her jacket. The sun is warm today. It casts golden beams of light across everything, including the ancient headstones lining the paths. "You know, kinda like how it felt when we went to the spot where the *Eastland* sank?"

"I love Déjà Vu!" Emily breaks into a skip. Her newly bobbed hair bounces wildly around her, and her tall, brown boots click against the pavement. Even in the middle of a grave-yard, she reminds me of a commercial for an energy drink or something. Running a finger over the bracelet she gave me, I smile. Emily was right. I survived. And thanks to the fact that Emily is finally starting to open up a little more about what's going on at home with her mom, so will she.

Warner turns to me. One perfect, dark eyebrow is raised. "Um, déjà vu? What's she talking about?"

"Lipstick," Casley answers with a smile. "Your cousin is *really* into lipstick."

"Most girls are," Warner fires back with a grin.

"Except for Claire," Sam says, chuckling. "Apparently our little science nerd is into graveyards now."

Everyone laughs except for me.

"Claire?" Warner says. The rest of the group pulls ahead, following behind a still-skipping Emily. "Something wrong?"

Is something wrong? I'm not sure. A month ago, I was terrified of Dad's books, stories, and tours. Now I'm walking through a graveyard.

Willingly.

With the guy I like.

"This is weird, isn't it?" I ask him. My voice is shaking, but I can't help it.

"What, being in a cemetery with you guys?" he asks. "Kinda. But it's weird in a good way. Like those blanket-sack thingies I see the infomercial for every Saturday morning. So comfy-looking, but so straaaange."

I snort-giggle, then cover my mouth. How embarrassing. Warner chuckles, and for the first time, I think I understand the whole "laughing with you, not at you" thing.

"Okay, then. You ready for this?"

He shoots me a skeptical look. "I'm not sure. I don't know what 'this' is just yet."

"Oh, I bet you do. Think hard," I respond.

Warner's mouth gapes open. "No way! Dexter Graves is actually buried in this cemetery?"

"Yeah. Why else would I bring you here?" I ask.

He shrugs. "I don't know. I didn't really think about that. Guess I didn't care."

Now it's my turn to laugh. "You didn't care that I dragged you to a graveyard after school?"

"Not really. I mean, I knew you'd be here, so it couldn't be all that bad."

I am so shocked I stumble over a small dip in the path. I did *not* just hear what I think I did…right?

"Claire! Warner! Hurry up, we found him!" Emily's voice pierces the silence between us.

I try to swallow through what feels like a lump of cat hair in my throat. "So, ah, I guess we better catch up."

"Guess so," he says softly. "Thanks for asking me to come. Your brother and Casley are cool."

"They are, aren't they?" I say. Pride swells in me. The old Claire—the one who was always afraid—can go dig a hole and jump in it, for all I care, because the new Claire has a pretty sweet life.

We walk over to where everyone else is standing. I sweep my arms over the statue they're gaping at. "Guys, meet Dexter."

Dropping my backpack on the ground, I dig around in it

until I find Dad's tattered copy of *Graveyards of Chicago*. "This statue was sculpted in 1844 by a man named Lorado Taft. He named it *Eternal Silence*."

"*Eternal Silence*," Casley repeats quietly, scowling as she eyes him. "Well, that's morbid."

"What did you want him to name it? *See Ya on the Flip Side*?" Sam asks, his deep laugh echoing through the otherwise silent graves.

She moves toward the statue cautiously, more like she's approaching a bear trap than a century-old gravesite. "Shut up, Sam! You know what I mean."

"Okay, okay. I was just kidding. Seriously, though. What's this guy's story?"

I can*not* believe I'm about to do this.

I imagine Dad here, the ghost glint he gets in his eyes. I think about how excited he always is to share these stories... this history. As warped and weird as it is, it's Chicago, and I really love Chicago.

"It's more of a legend," I begin in my most dramatic voice. "It says that anyone who dares to stand before Dexter and look into his eyes will see..."

"See what?" Emily interrupts. Her eyes are wider than Mom's giant Sunday-morning pancakes!

"A vision of their death!"

"Their death?" Emily nearly screams. All the color drains from her face, making her look more pale than usual. "Ohhhh no. No, thank you. Willie was enough. I'm all ghosted out."

I'm about remind her that it's only a legend when I notice Sam has gone quiet. He's watching Emily, too. Catching her eye, he grins, and she smiles back. Not a giant *I aced my history test* smile, but still one large enough to tell me that she might have an even bigger crush on Sam than he does on her.

"Huh," Warner says, like he's thinking out loud. "I'll try it. I've always been afraid it's going to be an elevator accident that takes me out. I'd love to know so I can keep taking the stairs if I'm right."

"Warner!" Emily snaps. "That's awful!"

Warner's mouth turns up into a lopsided grin. "Awww, you worried about me, Em?"

"Nope. Just don't wanna get stuck doing your chores if something happens to you," she fires back with a giggle.

"I'm with Emily," Casley says with a scowl. "I don't like this guy, Claire."

Once upon a time, I didn't like him, either. Dexter's statue is one of the scariest ones in the whole cemetery. The old Claire was afraid of ghosts and ghost stories. New Claire doesn't love them, but she isn't going to let them control her life, either. Not since Willie came along.

"Come on. This will be fun. It's just one eensy-weensy legend," I plead.

Emily springs to the front of our group. Her cheeks are flushed. "Fine. If we're actually going to do this, let's do it right. Make a line and hold hands."

Hold hands? I look over at Warner, and he shrugs like there's nothing we can do. But then I see him smile. Does he *want* to hold my hand? Do I want to hold his?

Sam clears his throat. I almost forgot that my brother was here with us. "All right," he replies. "Let's form a chain. The first one to break it or look away from Dexter's face owes everyone else a malt from Oberweis."

Casley rubs her hands together like a Disney villain. "Oh, I've *so* got this. I'll take strawberry. With whipped cream. Oh, and sprinkles."

"Puhhh-lease," Emily groans. "Just because I don't like this guy doesn't mean I can't stare into his stupid face for a minute."

"Then show us, hot stuff," Sam teases.

I sneak a glance at my brother, a smile perched on my lips. I won't tease him about his obvious crush on Emily now, but when we get home, all bets are off. But first, I've gotta win this bet. I love Oberweis. Especially Cubbie Crunch.

Reaching out, I grab Warner's hand. It isn't as scary as

I thought it would be. Actually, it's nice. Comfortable. Like it's something I've done a dozen times before. Only I haven't. Funny how life surprises you around every corner. My brother went from failing math to acing it. The perfect girls have the least perfect lives. The best friend who I thought was moving on isn't going anywhere. And the cutest boy in school, Warner Jameson, is holding my hand.

Wild.

Our entire group has finally formed a line and locked hands. I begin the countdown, enjoying the fact that for once, I'm not counting because I'm scared.

Three...

Two...

One...

As my eyes find Dexter's darkened face, I send a silent thank you up into the universe. To Willie. I don't know what kinds of visions my friends are seeing in this statue's face right now, but I know what I'm seeing. It's a kick-butt summer, followed by an even better eighth grade year.

A NOTE FROM THE AUTHOR

Friends,

I'm honored I had a chance to write this book, not only because I love scary stories, but also because I appreciate the opportunity to shed light on what some might call "forgotten" Chicago history. Events like the SS *Eastland* disaster affected my great city in a multitude of ways, yet the reality is that more than one hundred years later, many have never heard about it. Same with the Iroquois Theater fire. In the moments, hours, and days after the SS *Eastland* sank, the people of Chicago came together to save who they could, to clean up the aftermath, and ultimately, to grieve the 844 lives they lost. This unity reminds us that even though Chicago is a big city, it is still a community—a community that was forever changed in just twenty feet of water that tragic day in 1915.

If you'd like to read more about the SS *Eastland*, I would recommend the book *Capsized! The Forgotten Story of the SS*

Eastland Disaster by Patricia Sutton. The author has done a wonderful job of researching and detailing the event with quotes, photographs, and even trial transcripts. In addition, if you're ever in Chicago, you can visit the spot where the SS *Eastland* sank. There is a plaque along the riverfront, like the one described in *Scritch Scratch*, and inside the lobby of the Reid Murdoch building, there's a small exhibit. It's not as detailed as the exhibit at the Chicago History Museum, but it's still worth stopping by if you are in the area.

In addition, there are a few articles I read while researching for this book that I'd like to share with you. The first one, titled "Chicago Now Reunited Eastland Relative with the Past" is fascinating and includes more details about Willie Novotny and his family than most everything else I read. The article "The Eastland Disaster Killed More Passengers Than the Titanic and the Lusitania" from *Smithsonian Magazine* is also helpful. It features a timeline of what was happening in the brief time it took the boat to capsize. One last article to check out is "Eastland Disaster" from the Encyclopaedia Britannica, which includes an original video of the SS *Eastland* being pulled back out of the water after the accident, as well as some good explanations for why the ship sank to begin with. If you're still looking for more information on the sinking of the *Eastland* after these resources, great! Try the Eastland Disaster

Historical Society website (eastlanddisaster.org). It includes photos, videos, and descriptions of what happened that fateful day. There's even a camera you can use to view the location where the boat sank.

Also, if you're interested in learning about some locations mentioned in *Scritch Scratch*, I would recommend a trip to the Chicago History Museum. It's filled with amazing displays, and there's even a research room where you can dive deep into events like the Iroquois Theater fire, the removal of the old city cemetery in Lincoln Park, and landmarks like the Couch Tomb. Plus, museums are cool, so why not get to know one of the most incredible ones I've ever been to? Maybe, just maybe, you'll run into me while you're there. It *is* one of my favorite places to write, after all!

Stay brave, friends.

Best,

ACKNOWLEDGMENTS

Hi, friends! Thank you for reading Claire and Willie's story. I hope you enjoyed reading it as much as I enjoyed writing it. While I may have been the original creator of this story, in reality there is an entire team of people who worked very hard to make *Scritch Scratch* a reality. I'd like to take a moment to thank them, and I hope you'll continue reading so you know how many talented and passionate people it takes to bring a book into the world!

I'd like to start by thanking my family. They are my biggest support system. To my husband, John, and my kids, Rob, Ben, and Ella: you four are more of my writing process than you can imagine. I strive to instill your enthusiasm, your kindness, and your brilliance into my characters, and I channel your determination every time I begin drafting a new manuscript. So, thank you. Thank you for everything you do. I love you with all my heart.

I'd also like to thank my wonderful agent, Kathleen Rushall, for being the very best creative partner I could imagine. You see potential in everything, and I'm so grateful for your endless optimism and encouragement!

To Kate Prosswimmer, for originally acquiring this book—thank you. Your excitement made me fall in love with this story all over again. Because of your vision, *Scritch Scratch* found the perfect home.

A huge thank-you goes out to my editor, Annie Berger, and the entire team at Sourcebooks Kids. I can't express how wonderful every step of this process has been. From Annie's vision during the very first edit stage, all the way through the copyediting (thank you, Cassie Gutman and Sarah Kasman), I've felt supported. Thank you to Danielle McNaughton, who designed the internal template for this beautiful book, and art director Nicole Hower, for creating an absolutely glorious cover as well. And Travis Hasenour, the map is everything I could have wanted and more! I'm beyond impressed and grateful for all of your talent and enthusiasm.

Next, I'd like to thank my critique partners, Becky Wallace and Jenni Walsh, for their insight, patience, and kindness while helping me shape *Scritch Scratch* into something workable. You two are fabulous!

To the entire Spooky Middle-Grade crew—thank you! Thank you for cheering with me, for encouraging me while I write, and for being the kind of support group every writer should have. Hugs to each and every one of you.

Thanks to historian Adam Selzer, for once again helping during my research phase for this book, and for sparking the idea for the *Spirits* bus with his own amazing ghost tour!

There are some very important friends I've met over the years who I'd like to acknowledge for their constant love and support as well. To Nikki Mancini (who officially now has a character named after her!), thank you. Your encouragement means a lot, friend, and your students are so lucky to have you in their lives! Kristen Walsh and the students of Murphy Jr. High—you are AMAZING. From the mural you painted in your school to your warm welcome every time I come visit, I am blown away by your support. To Nancy Gadzala and the Title Squad at Madison School (Tess, Marin, Nina, Kate, Liam, Rutger, Nick, Landon, and Kaylee)—thank you! Your brainstorming session was incredible, and I'm so proud of each and every one of you for the ideas you came up with!

And to my incredible street team, thank you. There are people who believe street teams are a waste of time, but I say that's not true. My street team supported me. They encouraged me. And even more amazing, they connected me with new readers. I'll always be grateful.

Last, but definitely not least, thank you to my reader friends. Without you, I wouldn't be able to write *any* books. Your support is the greatest gift of all.

ABOUT THE AUTHOR

Lindsay Currie lives in Chicago, Illinois, with her high school sweetheart turned husband and their three amazing children. While she didn't go to school to be a historian, researching her city's complex, and often spooky history is one of Lindsay's favorite things to do—especially when there are ghost legends involved! If you'd like to find out what books Lindsay has coming out next and discover some fun, behind-the-scenes facts about her, like one of her favorite places to vacation (think mouse ears!), or what color hair she's always wanted to have, visit her website at lindsaycurrie.com.